Louisa May Alcott

Young Novelist

Illustrated by Meryl Henderson

Louisa May Alcott

Young Novelist

by Beatrice Gormley

ALADDIN PAPERBACKS

First Aladdin Paperbacks edition May 1999

Text copyright © 1999 by Beatrice Gormley
Illustrations copyright © 1999 by Meryl Henderson

Aladdin Paperbacks
An imprint of Simon & Schuster
Children's Publishing Division
1230 Avenue of the Americas
New York, NY 10020

The text for this book was set in New Caledonia.
The illustrations were rendered in pen and ink wash.
Printed and bound in the United States of America
10 9 8 7 6 5

Library of Congress Cataloging-in-Publication Data
Gormley, Beatrice.
Louisa May Alcott / by Beatrice Gormley ; illustrated by Meryl Henderson.
— 1st Aladdin Paperbacks ed.
p.   cm.
Summary: Traces the life of the author of the well-loved stories of the March
sisters, *Little Women* and their sequels.
ISBN 0-689-82025-9 (pbk.)
1. Alcott, Louisa May, 1832-1888—Childhood and youth—Juvenile literature.
2. Women authors, American—19th century—Biography—Juvenile literature.
3. Concord (Mass.)—Social life and customs—Juvenile literature. [1. Alcott,
Louisa May, 1832-1888. 2. Authors, American. 3. Women—Biography.]
I. Henderson, Meryl, ill. II. Title.
PS1018G47   1999
813'.4—dc21
[b]   98-30236
CIP   AC

Illustrations

Contents

Louisa May Alcott

Young Novelist

Two Birthdays

One summer day in the year 1835, the Common in Boston was dotted with families enjoying the fine weather. Bronson and Abby Alcott sat under a tree by the Frog Pond with their three little girls: Anna, Louisa (nicknamed Louy), and the new baby, Lizzie. Gentlemen in top hats and ladies in bonnets and sweeping skirts strolled along the curving paths of the park, while children climbed trees and sailed toy boats in the pond.

Bronson Alcott's hat lay beside him on the grass, and the dappled sunlight shone on his blond hair. He leaned on one elbow, his long legs stretched out, while he read aloud from a book. Lively expressions played over Abby Alcott's strong features as she listened to him. She cradled the baby in her arms, and beside her Anna cradled her rag doll.

But Louy was too restless to sit still. She wandered around the tree, stooping on the other side to pick up a broad leaf. The breeze lifted her dark curly hair as she gazed out over the pond. Light danced on the water, and wavelets rocked the boats. Papa could make a boat out of a leaf, but he was busy.

"Stay close by, Louy," said her mother as the little girl carried her leaf toward the pond. Louy didn't answer, because one especially beautiful toy boat with four masts caught her eye. It looked just like the big ships Marmee had shown her in Boston Harbor. Its miniature sails puffed out as it glided over the ripples.

Without noticing, Louy dropped her leaf at

the muddy edge of the pond. The beautiful ship was sailing right toward her, closer, closer. "Oh," breathed Louy, reaching out to catch it.

Then the breeze turned. The ship hesitated, its sails trembling, and slowly backed away from the bank. "Don't go!" shouted Louy. She grabbed at a mast, missed, grabbed again—and fell right off the bank.

Louy seemed to hang in the air over the pond, helpless, for a long time. Then the water smacked her face and closed over her head. She couldn't see or breathe or call for help. Papa! she thought. Marmee!

But now something was pulling the back of her frock, hauling her up. She choked, sputtered, and blinked. Water streamed over her eyes, out of her nose and mouth. Someone set her down on her hands and knees beside the pond.

"My darling! Are you all right?" Marmee's arms were around her wet, muddy child. She

turned to the boy who had pulled Louy out of the pond. "How can I thank you? God bless you for saving my little girl!"

The boy's face and hands were the color of chocolate, Louy noticed. His teeth were very white as he smiled and shrugged.

Mr. Alcott wrapped his coat around shivering Louy and carried her home, and Mrs. Alcott walked alongside with Anna and the baby. Somehow they had all gotten wet and muddy, although only Louy had fallen in the pond.

That evening at supper, the Alcotts were still talking about Louy falling in the Frog Pond and the black boy pulling her out. "To think that people like that kind lad can be *owned*," said Abby, her dark eyes flashing. "Bought and sold like animals!"

"It is a terrible wrong. A shame to our nation," agreed Bronson. "But many of us are working for the cause of abolition. Your brother Sam's house is a stop on the

Underground Railroad. William Lloyd Garrison is risking his life by speaking out against slavery—that mob who dragged him through the streets meant to kill him."

Louy and Anna listened wide-eyed, and Louy struggled to understand. A railroad ran underground and stopped right at Uncle Sam's house. Bad men wanted to kill Mr. Garrison. People could be *owned*, the way a wagon driver owned his horse. It didn't make any sense.

"Slavery is an evil institution," Bronson Alcott went on. "It cannot, *will* not, last." His voice was calm, but there was a determined look in his blue eyes.

The summer passed, and now Mr. Alcott and Anna, who was five, left every morning for the school where Bronson Alcott taught. Louy liked having Mrs. Alcott sing and play games with only her, except that Marmee spent too much time with Baby Lizzie. Every day the Alcotts took a walk around the Common. The trees turned from green to yellow and orange, and then the branches were bare, showing the gold dome of the State House on the hill above the park.

Then, on a frosty November morning, the special day arrived. Abby Alcott dressed Louy, as well as Anna, in a shawl and bonnet, and she put on her own wraps. Lizzie was to stay home with the landlady, Mrs. Beach, but Abby and Louy were to go to school with Bronson and Anna.

As they walked from Mrs. Beach's boardinghouse through the narrow streets of Boston, past brick houses and shops, Anna and Louy each held one of their mother's hands. Their tall, lean father strode in front of them, a top hat on his blond head. He kept turning to smile at his wife and daughters.

Louy was three years old. Well, three years old *tomorrow*, she corrected herself. But today she was going to Papa's school! The thought of it made the little girl skip on the cobblestones. School was a longer walk from home than King's Chapel, the old stone church where Marmee took the girls on Sundays.

But here was the really exciting thing about today: the whole school would celebrate Louisa May Alcott's birthday. Hers and Papa's—they had both been born on November 29.

"Marmee," Anna was saying to Abby Alcott, "do you remember when Louy got lost on the steamboat? They found her down below, all dirty."

Louy wanted to pull her sister's hair for bringing up that story again. Instead, she stuck out her tongue at Anna behind Marmee's back. "I wasn't lost on the steamboat." She had climbed down to the engine room on purpose, because it was noisy and exciting there. "Besides, I was only two."

"Anna—Louisa," said their mother in a

warning tone. "Here's the school, just ahead." She nodded up the street toward a building with towers, four stories high. The entrance was a tall pointed arch.

Father, turning again, stooped to face the girls. His deep-set eyes, gazing into theirs, were very blue. "My girls want to please me on this special day, don't they? How can they best please me?"

"By being cheerful and kind to everyone," said Anna, giving the expected answer.

Louy was struck with remorse. How could she be angry with her sister on such a happy day? "I love everyone!" she exclaimed. "Even Baby Lizzie."

They climbed the four flights of stairs to Bronson Alcott's school, up on the top floor of the Masonic Temple. The main room was almost as grand as King's Chapel. Light streamed through the arched window onto globes and sculptures of famous men and whole shelves of books.

"Look, Papa!" exclaimed Anna. "The school is decorated with flowers—and see the bowls of apples and pears."

The pupils were waiting, sitting in a half circle facing Mr. Alcott's desk. They all loved Papa, of course, thought Louy. She could tell by the eager way they gazed at him. Elizabeth Peabody, Papa's assistant, also gazed at him with eager, trusting eyes.

As the school day began, Miss Peabody, her hair a little untidy and her clothes a little rumpled, rustled around the room helping the children and taking notes. Baby Lizzie was named after her, Louy knew.

The other girls and boys must have been excited about the celebration, too, but they read quietly in their seats. Louy, being extra good today, walked softly across the floor and looked at the globes and the sculptures until the clock struck ten. Now, the celebration would begin!

The pupils hurried to bring out wreaths of

flowers and laurel leaves, and they crowned Louy and Mr. Alcott. A boy gave a speech, telling how much the pupils loved the school. Mr. Alcott gave a long speech, telling how he had grown up on a farm in Connecticut. His family was poor and he had hardly any schooling. But his mother taught him to read and write, and encouraged him to love books.

A girl recited a birthday poem, and finally it was time for the birthday refreshments. Louy, the birthday girl, would have the honor of giving them out. Papa lifted her onto a table, and Marmee handed her a plate of little raisin cakes, one for each child.

The cakes were so close that Louy could smell their sugary, buttery, spicy scent, but she didn't grab. She was old enough to wait until everyone else had one. She beamed with pride as each boy or girl came up to take a cake and said, "Thank you, Louisa."

But now only one cake was left. There had been a terrible mistake. Louy looked from the single raisin cake on the plate to the last girl waiting her turn. She pulled the plate away from the girl's reaching hand. "It's mine. It's *my* birthday!"

Louy was taking a deep breath to shout when she felt her mother's hand on her shoulder. Marmee's voice spoke in her ear: "I know my Louy will not let her little friend go without."

Louy looked up at Marmee, then at the other girl. She looked at the cake, dotted with delicious raisins. Biting her lip, she held out the plate and watched the girl take the last cake.

Marmee gave her a hug and a kiss. "That's my dear!"

Louy didn't cry. She was proud that she had done the right thing. Still—she wished she had the cake.

Wild Louy

Bronson Alcott's Temple School was a big success. It was different from any other school at this time, because the teachers didn't punish the children to make them learn. At other schools, the children hated their lessons. But Mr. Alcott believed that if he treated the children with respect, they would naturally enjoy learning.

Bronson Alcott didn't punish children for misbehaving, either. At least, he didn't punish in the usual way. One night in bed, Anna told Louy the story of how Papa had dealt with two unruly boys.

"Papa picked up his ruler and took them out in the hall," Anna whispered. "They didn't mind, because they thought he would just give them a little smack on their hands."

"What happened?" urged Louy. "Did he *hit* them?"

"No." Anna paused to let the suspense build up. "He made them hit *him*. They begged not to, but he made them do it. They cried." She sniffled herself, at the thought of anyone hitting Papa. Louy knew she would cry, too, if she were punished that way.

With the school going so well, the Alcotts could move from Mrs. Beach's boardinghouse to a big rented house on Front Street. Now they had plenty of room. There was a study for Mr. Alcott, a parlor with a Franklin stove for Mrs. Alcott to show off to guests, and a garden in the back for the girls to play in. There was a room, too, for Miss Peabody, Bronson's assistant. Abby Alcott happily took in students from the school as boarders, welcomed friends and relatives, and hired servants to help her with all the work.

The Alcotts were still near enough to the Boston Common to go there almost every day, even when there was snow on the ground. The great gold dome of the State House gleamed through the bare trees as Louy and Anna skipped ahead of their parents. Boys coasted down the Long Slide at the edge of the park—and so did reckless Louy.

In the spring the girls ran and played and fell down on the Common's wide stretches of grass. Many children had hoops to drive along the paths. Anna had a hoop, too, but it kept wobbling away from her and falling over. Louy could drive it farther than her older sister could. The Common also had low-branched trees, good for climbing, and Louy wasn't afraid to climb right up to the top.

When Bronson Alcott was home, his favorite place was his study. It was Louy's favorite *inside* place, too. While Papa sat at his desk and read or wrote, Louy and Anna played on the carpet. They built a bridge with books and danced around it, singing, "London Bridge is falling down!" The books made lovely thumps at the end of the song, when Louy pushed them over.

But books were more than building blocks. There were stories, wonderful stories, hidden inside them. If Louy learned to read as well as Papa, he promised her, she could find the stories for herself. She would even be able to *write* stories.

One day, while their father read to himself with a dreamy look on his face, Anna and Louy were building towers. But Louy got bored with building, and she opened one of the books. It had nice wide blank margins. Maybe she could write a story *now*. Taking a pencil, she scrawled marks up one side of a page and down the other.

"Louisa!" Papa had just noticed what she was doing. "What made you scribble in Plutarch's *Lives*? Anna has never done such a thing."

Anna, smiling slightly at Louy, placed another book on her tower.

"You must learn your letters, Louy," decided Bronson Alcott. "Then you can truly write, instead of playing at it and ruining books."

Lessons with Papa were always fun. He got down on the carpet with the girls and bent his long, thin body into the shapes of letters. Lying on his back, he stretched his legs and arms up to make the letter V. Then he grasped his ankles to make a circle the letter O, like the hoop Louy drove around the Common.

Next, Bronson let Anna and Louy take turns dipping his pen in the ink bottle. They practiced making letters on the pages of his journal until their fingers were cramped.

"Read a story, Papa," begged Anna finally. "Read about the Pilgrim."

"And the monster," added Louy, with an enjoyable shudder.

So Bronson took the red book, *Pilgrim's Progress*, down from the bookshelf. On the cover there was a picture in gilt of an angel lifting up a knight in armor, the Pilgrim. There were only a few pictures inside the book, but the words Papa read made even better pictures in Louy's mind. She could see the monster blocking the Pilgrim's way. It had scales like a fish, wings like a dragon, claws like a bear, and a hideous roar.

The Pilgrim was on a long, hard journey, and it often seemed that he would never reach the Heavenly City. When he finally did, at the end of the story, Louy could imagine the city shining before him. It was brighter than the gold dome of the State House near the Boston Common.

28

❈ ❈ ❈

"Not today, Louy," said Abby Alcott. She pulled a clean pink frock over Louy's head. "Lizzie must take a nap this afternoon. We won't have time to walk to the Common."

"But *I* have time," thought Louy. "I won't bother Marmee about it anymore."

A few minutes later, her mother was busy changing Lizzie. Helpful Anna folded the clean diaper. Louy tiptoed down the back stairs.

Out in the yard, the woman who helped Mrs. Alcott with the heavy housework was pumping water into a bucket. But her back was turned, and she didn't see Louy slip around the corner of the house to the street.

There! Louy was out of the house, all by herself. Now, anything could happen. Her heart beat faster as she ran down their little street to the main road.

Louy was all by herself and ready for adventures, like the Pilgrim. No scaly monsters or shining angels were in sight yet—only a streetcar full of men in top hats, a workman pushing a handcart full of bricks, and a carriage pulled by four horses, with a little girl holding her doll up to the carriage window.

Louy's stomach growled, and she remembered that she hadn't had lunch yet. Maybe she would go back home to eat, and have adventures later. Then she noticed three boys coming out of a ramshackle boardinghouse. They were all freckled faced and blue eyed. The biggest one carried a hoop.

"I can drive a hoop around the Common," Louy told him.

"Prove it, then," he challenged her.

"That's where we're going, to the Common," added one of the other boys. "Want to come?"

"Of course I do," said Louy, "but I'm hungry."

Now that they thought of it, the boys were hungry, too. Patrick, the biggest, sent one of his younger brothers into the house for food.

Sitting down on the front steps, Louy and the boys shared potatoes and salt fish.

Then they set off on the long walk to the Common. Louy didn't think about how long it was, though, because they stopped on the way and rummaged through some interesting trash heaps. Then they played follow the leader the rest of the way. At the park, they spent a glorious afternoon driving the hoop, playing tag, and making leaf boats to sail on the pond.

But when the boys decided to go home, Louy was still busy running around the pond. "Good-bye, then," said Patrick. Louy, trying to steer the leaf boats by puffing at them, hardly noticed.

The next time Louy looked up from the water, the boys were nowhere around. The sun was low in the sky, giving a pinkish tinge to the gilded dome of the State House. Louy began walking, but she couldn't remember how she had gotten to the park with the boys.

She walked and walked, turning one corner after another, but nothing looked familiar.

Her legs aching, Louy stopped to watch a lamplighter work. At each lamppost, he reached up to light the wick. The glow from a lamppost near Louy fell on a doorway, and Louy saw a big, shaggy black dog sitting on the top step.

"Hello, doggy," said Louy. "Are you lonely?" The dog wagged his tail. That meant yes, she decided. "Don't be lonely." She climbed the steps and gave him a hug, and he licked her face. She would stay with him for a while, to keep him company. She rested her head on his back.

The next thing Louy knew, a bell was ringing nearby. It was the town crier, getting people's attention for his news. "Lost!" he shouted. "Little girl—pink frock, white hat—"

The big dog and Louy both jumped up from the doorstep. "That's me!" Louy shouted.

The town crier took Louy home, stopping at his house on the way to feed her bread and molasses. She was still having a good time until they reached the Alcotts' front door, and she saw Marmee's and Papa's faces.

They hugged her, but Abby Alcott scolded and cried at the same time. Bronson, for once, had lost his calm expression. The house was dark, except for the light in the front hall, and Anna and Lizzie were nowhere to be seen. It was very late, Louy realized.

Stooping in front of Louy, her father fixed her with his reproachful blue eyes. "Louy, why are you so wild?" he asked. "Your sister Anna is good and obedient. And Lizzie is a little angel."

The next day, Mrs. Alcott took no chances. She tied Louy, by a rope around her waist, to the arm of the sofa. When Marmee was out of earshot, Anna said to Louy, "You must be a dog—a bad runaway dog."

"Just you wait, Anna," growled Louy. But

she was ashamed to be tied up like an animal.

Why hadn't Anna ever thought of running away? Why didn't Baby Lizzie mind being cooped up, either? One time Louy and Anna had built a castle of books in the study around Lizzie, and then they ran outside to play and forgot. Lizzie was trapped, but she didn't even cry. She just went to sleep in her book prison, and Marmee had found her there much later.

Louy remembered Papa's question last night. Why *was* she so wild?

Little Pilgrims

In the Temple School days, everyone was happy. Bronson Alcott loved teaching children. Important people, including the writer and philosopher Ralph Waldo Emerson and his influential friends, were impressed with his ideas about human nature and education. Abby Alcott believed in her husband, and she was proud of him. Elizabeth Peabody, Bronson's assistant, almost worshiped him.

Mrs. Alcott's father, Colonel Joseph May, was also happy with his son-in-law. Colonel May was well-known and respected in Boston, and he had often had doubts about Bronson, the poor self-educated farm boy turned philosopher. But now Bronson Alcott was a respected citizen of Boston, too. And he was earning good money to support his family.

When Abby Alcott took her three girls to visit her father in his house on Washington Street, they were fascinated with their grandfather May. "Grandfather looks like Marmee," whispered Louy to Anna, as their mother showed the old man Baby Lizzie. He had a long nose like Marmee's, and his black eyes gave the same sharp glance.

"*I* think he looks like a mixture of Marmee and President George Washington," giggled Anna. Although the Revolutionary War had ended fifty years ago, Grandfather May still dressed in knee breeches and buckled shoes, and he wore his long hair tied at the back of his neck.

Louy liked that visit with Grandfather May, and the many visits afterward.

Grandfather told stories about the old days of the American Revolution. He served the nicest cakes for tea, and sometimes he gave the girls pretty new dresses to take home. He did scold Louy once for hanging a doll out the window with no clothes on, but he still seemed to like her.

Yes, everyone was happy—for a while. Then one evening at the Alcotts' dinner table, Louy sensed something different. What was it?

Mr. Alcott was at the head of the table as usual, and Mrs. Alcott at the other end with Lizzie's high chair next to her. Elizabeth Peabody sat on one side, Anna and Louy on the other. Maybe the change was that there was no meat on the table. Papa had decided it was wrong to kill animals.

No, it was Miss Peabody who seemed different tonight. As she tucked her straggly hair behind her ears, she was looking at Mr. Alcott in a different way. Before, she had always gazed at him admiringly, or beamed and nodded as he spoke. Tonight, she looked mistrustful, as if she wondered what he would do next. Was Miss Peabody upset at not having meat for dinner?

Louy took a bite of mashed potatoes, rich with melted butter. She didn't mind not eating meat when the vegetables were so good. And Marmee and the girls still ate eggs and milk and pie and cake, although Papa had decided to give up those foods.

That evening was only the first hint of trouble. Soon there seemed to be sparks in the air at the Alcotts' dinner table, like the sparks that crackled off the cat's fur in dry weather. Only the sparks flew between Miss Peabody and Mr. and Mrs. Alcott.

"People are spreading rumors about your school," said Elizabeth Peabody to Bronson Alcott one night. "Do you think it is wise to talk to the pupils about subjects that upset the parents so much?"

Miss Peabody had criticized Papa! Louy and Anna stared at her with their forks halfway to their mouths. Louy wondered what "subjects" she meant, but she didn't get any clues from Marmee or Papa. Mr. Alcott's expression turned blank, and he acted as if he hadn't heard Miss Peabody at all. Mrs. Alcott's face reddened, and her dark eyes sparkled angrily. They both ignored Miss Peabody for the rest of the meal.

After dinner, Louy questioned Anna. Anna hated to say anything bad about Papa, but she admitted that *something* was wrong. Some children had left the Temple School, and there were rumors in school that their parents were angry. She thought the trouble had to do with Papa talking to the children about how babies were born.

"But why would that upset them?" Louy was mystified.

Anna didn't know. She'd heard what Papa said in school, about love, and roses blooming, and sunshine on the garden soil making seeds sprout. But she hadn't understood what it had to do with babies, and she didn't think the other boys and girls had, either.

Not long after that, Elizabeth Peabody was gone—gone from the Temple School, and gone from the Alcotts' house. "To think that I named Baby Lizzie after that woman!" Louy heard her mother say. "From now on, our girl will be Elizabeth *Sewall* Alcott."

At first Louy thought Miss Peabody had caused all the trouble, and now everything would be fine again. Mr. Alcott hired a new assistant, the beautiful Margaret Fuller. Louisa thought she was a wonderful teacher. But the parents of Mr. Alcott's pupils were angrier than ever, and almost all of them took their children out of the Temple School. Louy heard that people were saying terrible things about her father. "Filthy and godless," one newspaper called his teaching. He was "insane or half-witted," another newspaper said.

With hardly any money coming in, Bronson Alcott had to move his few remaining pupils, including Anna and Louisa, into a dark little basement room. And the Alcotts had to give up the big house on Front Street. They moved into a tiny cramped house in the South End of Boston. They were poor.

Uncle Sam May sent the Alcotts a barrel of potatoes or a crate of apples whenever he could, and Ralph Emerson gave them money now and then. But Colonel May sent nothing. "Why can't we visit Grandfather?" Louy asked her mother. "He had such nice cakes."

Mrs. Alcott only shook her head, her lips setting in a tight line. Anna explained to Louy later, "Marmee and Grandfather quarreled, because Grandfather blames Papa. He thinks if only Papa had been sensible, he wouldn't have lost the school. Of course Marmee can't speak to him, when he talks about Papa like that."

When Louy was almost six, the Alcotts

moved again, to share a house on Beach Street with their friends the Russells. Bronson Alcott started a new school, which he taught at home. Their parlor was a much nicer classroom than the basement room at the Masonic Temple, Louy thought. There were many new pupils besides Anna and Louy.

The Alcotts felt cheerful again. Soon there would be another baby in the family—a brother, Louy hoped. In the spring her wish came true, but in a sad way: The baby boy died the same day it was born.

Late that spring, a girl named Susan Robinson joined Mr. Alcott's school. To Louy and Anna she was just another little girl, nothing special about her. But she was black, like the boy who had pulled Louisa out of Frog Pond a couple of years ago.

Only a week or so after Susan started at the school, one of the parents, Dr. Flint, paid a visit to Bronson Alcott. Dr. Flint's face was grim under his top hat, and he did not stay long. Afterward, Louy heard Mr. Alcott tell his wife, "He spoke for all the parents. They demand that I expel Susan Robinson from the school."

"Surely you didn't agree to such a wicked demand!" exclaimed Abby Alcott.

"I did not," said Bronson. His calm blue eyes met her passionate dark eyes, and Louy understood that her mother and father had done something very brave. It seemed that a black child in the school made people even angrier than teaching how babies were born.

Within a week or so, Bronson Alcott's new school had scattered, the way a flock of pigeons on the Common scattered when Louy ran at them. All the new pupils, except Susan and the Russell children, were gone. The Alcotts were poor again. A man with a hard face began to come to their door and say that Mr. Alcott had to pay the money he owed. Louy could see that Marmee was ashamed to be in debt.

Sometimes at night, when Louy was supposed to be asleep, she heard her mother and father quarreling about money. Marmee said that Papa owed *six thousand dollars* he couldn't pay back. Anna didn't believe Louisa, when she told her the next morning. "Not Papa!"

"But if Marmee said it," argued Louy, "it must be true."

One day Louy asked her father, "We're in the Slough of Despond now, aren't we, Papa?" He was reading to the girls from *Pilgrim's Progress* again. The Pilgrim was struggling through a slough, a low place full of scum and filth and mire.

"Yes, my dear." Bronson Alcott's blue eyes, which looked sad and anxious these days, beamed at Louy. "You understand, don't you? Our life is a journey, just as it is for the Pilgrim. Sometimes it will be a happy, easy journey through meadows and flowers and sunshine, with many good friends to help us along. But sometimes it will be a hard, miserable way. And people we thought were our friends will try to keep us from our goal."

At least one friend, Ralph Emerson, was faithful. He still invited Bronson to his home in Concord, and he still came to visit the Alcotts in Boston.

Fortunately Grandfather May, too, was on good terms with the Alcotts again. Even though he was disappointed with Bronson Alcott as a son-in-law, he was too old and lonely to let that stand between him and Abby, his favorite daughter. Louy was glad to visit her grandfather again, although he was quite deaf now. She had to shout in his ear.

On Louy's seventh birthday, her mother gave her a doll. Louy had never asked for a doll, although Anna loved hers dearly. Anna always sat quietly, Louy noticed, when she played with her doll. Besides, Louy's favorite

kind of playmates—boys—did not play with dolls.

Louy read the birthday note Marmee had written her. "My dear little girl," it began. Mrs. Alcott hoped the doll would be a "quiet playmate" for Louy. "Be a kind mama, and love her for my sake."

Louy looked from the doll, staring at her with a silly blank expression, to her mother. Abby Alcott's dark eyes were warm with love for her. "I do love my doll, Marmee!" She hugged and kissed her mother, and then planted a kiss on the doll's face. She would do anything her mother wanted, even play with dolls.

But Louy quickly discovered that dolls could be fun. You didn't *have* to play so quietly with them. Anna's and Louy's dolls began to have adventures, like the Pilgrim. They fell into a slough full of mud. They wandered into the woods by themselves and got lost and very scared before Louy and Anna rescued them.

Dolls could even die tragically and be buried with grand ceremonies. And then the next day, the same dolls were alive and ready to play with again. Anna was more fun, too, thought Louy, when they played make-believe with their dolls.

One afternoon, when Ralph Emerson was visiting, he and Bronson took a long walk around the city, talking the whole time. Then Bronson and Ralph and Abby had tea in the parlor, while the girls played on the carpet. Ralph Emerson smiled at the Alcotts. "Won't you move to Concord, at last?" he asked. "Our little river would run gentler and our meadows look greener to me, if such a thing could be."

Louy stopped playing to listen. She had heard Mr. Emerson ask the same question before, but her parents had always quickly said no. Now, her father was rubbing his chin thoughtfully. "The countryside has its attrac-tions," he admitted. "Instead of depending on other people's money, I could make my living from the very earth."

"Precisely!" said Mr. Emerson. "You'd be the philosopher at the plow."

"We could have cows and geese and cats and dogs and horses!" Louy joined in. She loved animals.

"And dear baby lambs," added Anna.

"No, no," said Bronson Alcott, gently but firmly. "We would not raise animals." He had already explained to the girls that he felt it was wrong to take milk from a cow or wool from a sheep or eggs from a chicken.

"Lambies," said little Lizzie happily.

"*You* are my lambie angel," teased Mr. Alcott, picking Lizzie up. Louy watched, thinking that *she* was not any kind of an angel. She never had been, and never would be.

"I don't know," said Abby Alcott slowly. "We'd need money to move out to Concord. Of course, my father might help us with the expenses. And maybe my brother Sam could

50

spare some money. But—to leave all my friends and family in the city! It's such a long trip to Concord—three hours by stage-coach."

"But we'd have our friends in Concord." Bronson's blue eyes were glowing, as they did when an idea caught him up.

"Indeed you would," said Ralph Emerson.

Concord

The day of April 1, 1840, was suddenly cold in Concord, Massachusetts. Louy and her sisters had pink noses and numb fingers, but they didn't care. "This is our new house!" shouted Louy. She led Anna and Lizzie at a run through one room after the other of the rambling brown cottage. Papa had named it "Dove Cottage."

The Alcotts' new home was a small house on the farm of Edmund Hosmer, a friend of Ralph Emerson's. Mr. Emerson had paid the rent, happy that the Alcotts would now be within walking distance of his house on the Lexington Turnpike.

Outside the cottage, the world sparkled like fairyland, with ice on every twig and blade of grass. Mr. Alcott's blue eyes sparkled, too, as he gazed around. "I'll put the vegetable garden there . . . and the apple orchard over there . . . and the barn needs some repairs and whitewash . . ." He beamed at Mrs. Alcott.

Abby Alcott beamed back at her husband. "A house of our own!"

As Bronson threw himself into planting the garden, Abby threw herself into cleaning their new home and sewing curtains. She sang loud, cheerful hymns as she worked. "Arise, my soul, stretch every nerve, and press with vigor on," she warbled. It lifted Louy's heart to hear her.

Louy had lived in the city all her life, except for summer visits to Uncle Sam's house in Scituate. Here in Concord she had

room to run through fields and woods, over hills and along rivers, around ponds. And there were plenty of playmates, with the large Hosmer family next door. Louy and Cyrus Hosmer, both daredevils, hit it off immediately. They proceeded to risk their necks together, climbing trees and jumping from the barn beams.

Since Mr. Alcott did not keep farm animals, the Alcott and Hosmer children could have the whole barn for themselves. It was perfect for hide-and-seek on rainy days. But the most fun was putting on plays.

Louy was always the director and the star. In the fairy tale "Jack and the Beanstalk," she was the hero Jack. "You be Jack's mother, Anna," she ordered. "Lizzie, you be the cow. We can tie a long squash vine to the ladder, to make the beanstalk."

The younger Hosmer children, sitting in the audience, held their breaths as Jack climbed the "beanstalk" to the giant's castle in the loft. They screamed with excitement when the giant fell from the "beanstalk" onto a pile of hay.

Pilgrim's Progress made an even better play. The children all put packs on their backs and took walking sticks. Louy led them up and down hills, through swamps and woods, and at last up the stairs of Dove Cottage to the "Heavenly City."

These days Mr. Alcott worked from dawn to dark on his small farm, and he had little time to teach his children. Anna started school at the Concord Academy, run by John and Henry Thoreau. Louy and Lizzie began walking to the Emersons' every day, to attend a little school taught by Miss Mary Russell, a friend of Mrs. Emerson's.

Louy loved going to the Emersons' spacious, peaceful house for any reason. When she had a chance, she peeped into Mr. Emerson's study on the first floor. Bookshelves lined the walls—Louy had never seen so many books. In the middle of the room, Mr. Emerson himself sat at his round desk, writing or reading.

That Fourth of July, a sweltering hot day, the Alcotts joined the celebration in the center of Concord. There was a parade with the music of fifes and drums, and the crack of rifles fired into the sky. The crowds shouted. "Hurrah!" shouted Louy with them, proud to be an American. William Henry Harrison, nicknamed "Tippecanoe," was running for president that year, and banners in the parade proclaimed the campaign slogan: "Tippecanoe and Tyler Too."

At the end of July, a new baby was born to the Alcotts. Again Louy hoped for a brother, but instead it was another sister, Abbie May.

"Doesn't she look like Papa?" said Anna. "Pink skin, blue eyes, blond hair." Anna liked taking care of the baby, as if she were a doll. Louy preferred helping her mother in the kitchen.

❀ ❀ ❀

Of all the new people the Alcotts met in Concord, the most unusual was Henry Thoreau. He was a young friend of Mr. Emerson's, a writer and a philosopher like Ralph Emerson and Bronson Alcott. Henry and Bronson struck up a friendship, too, and spent long hours talking.

The Alcott children also liked Henry Thoreau, this short, homely young man with the big nose. He knew the woods and fields and rivers "like a fox or a bird," Mr. Emerson remarked admiringly. Louy and her sisters followed Henry through thickets and into marshes, trying to be as silent and patient as he was. He would let them gaze through his spyglass at a hawk floating overhead, or have them help him press wildflowers, or point out an otter's tracks on the riverbank.

That fall, only six months after Bronson Alcott had begun his new life as a philosopher-farmer, the Alcotts were worried about money again. Bronson's crops had done well, and they had plenty of potatoes and turnips and beets and squash to eat with their boiled rice and whole wheat bread. But they still needed money for rent, for firewood, for the clothes the children kept growing out of. Ralph Emerson was so worried about the Alcotts, he invited them to move into the Emersons' house.

But Abby Alcott wouldn't hear of it. "I'll take in sewing," she said. "Anna is already a little seamstress, and Louy is handy with a needle, too." In the long evenings of the Massachusetts winter, Mrs. Alcott and the two older girls sat around the fire and sewed shirts, pillowcases, and hand towels for their wealthy friends in Boston.

In February 1841, Abby Alcott got word that Grandfather May was dying. She took Baby Abbie May and went to Boston to see him for the last time. Louy missed her mother badly, but it helped to write letters.

As she dipped her pen in the inkwell and scratched words across the paper, she felt as if Marmee were there, and they were talking. "I hope you will come home soon. . . . I want to see you and baby."

Since the Alcotts needed money so much, they thought that Abby's father would be generous to her in his will. But when the will was read, she was horribly hurt and disappointed. Her inheritance was only a modest sum, and it seemed it might have to go to pay off part of Bronson's six thousand dollars of debt.

At Thanksgiving, Abby Alcott's Aunt Hannah came to visit. After kissing Abby and all the girls, Aunt Hannah brought out a bag of hand-me-down clothes. "You dear creature!" said Mrs. Alcott. "It's like Christmas, isn't it, girls?"

Anna and Louy and Lizzie crowded around to see what would come out of the bag. There were dresses and aprons for the older girls, and a length of nice flannel to make frocks for Abbie May. "And shoes!" exclaimed Louy as several pairs fell out of the bag. The shoes she was wearing, handed down from Anna, pinched her toes, and the soles were as thin as paper. Marmee put an arm around Louy's shoulders, and Louy glanced up at her mother's happy face.

Then she noticed Aunt Hannah looking down, and she followed her gaze to Abby Alcott's feet. "Why, *Marmee*'s the one who needs shoes," thought Louy. Her mother's stockinged toes stuck right out of the worn leather.

Bronson Alcott had been watching the opening of the bag from his armchair, with a serene smile. "Didn't I tell you not to be anxious?" he said to his wife. Louy saw Aunt Hannah give Papa a look.

Later that day, the Alcotts took a Thanksgiving package of food to an even poorer family in Concord. The mother had four children, and the father had deserted them. Louy thought proudly, "We're poor, but we can still help other people. And we love each other."

For some time Mr. Alcott had been writing letters to England, and a stream of letters flowed from England to Dove Cottage in Concord. There was a group of people in England, one of them named Charles Lane, who thought Bronson Alcott was the greatest educator in the world. They admired his philosophy of education so much that they had named their school in England after him. "They want me to visit," Bronson told his wife in a tone of longing.

Of course the Alcotts had no money to pay his fare. But Ralph Emerson, always the good friend to the rescue, took up a collection. He called it the "Alcott-Voyage Fund." In May 1842, Bronson kissed Abby and Anna and Louy and Lizzie and Abbie May good-bye. He would be gone for six months.

The Newness

The same spring that Father left for England, Louy wrote her first poem. It was a day when the snow was almost gone, showing patches of green. That morning Louy had found a half-dead robin outside the back doorway. "Look, Anna—Lizzie! The poor thing."

They brought the bird into the kitchen, let him warm up near the stove, and offered him water and crumbs of bread. The girls admired his brick-red chest and yellow bill. When the bird had recovered, they let him out the back door and watched him hop over the new grass. Then he flew up into a nearby apple tree. The white apple blossoms hid the robin, but they heard his song: *Cheerup, cheerio!*

All that morning, Louy felt that her own chest was full of a song she wanted to let out. After the midday dinner, she didn't go right out to play. She found a piece of paper and pen and ink and sat down in a quiet corner. Words had been growing in her mind like new grass in the spring sunlight. She scribbled the words as fast as she could push the scratchy pen:

To the First Robin

Welcome, welcome, little stranger;

Fear no harm, and fear no danger . . .

It took Louy only a few minutes to finish eight lines. She ran with the poem to her mother, who was kneading bread dough in the kitchen. "Listen, Marmee!" She read it aloud.

"You will be a second Shakespeare!" exclaimed Mrs. Alcott. She smiled at Louy over the kitchen table. Louy knew that her mother was half joking, because William Shakespeare was the greatest genius of a writer that the world had ever known. But she was also half serious.

June and July were months of birthdays— first Lizzie's, then Abbie May's. For Lizzie's seventh birthday, Mrs. Alcott and Louy and Anna draped the inside of one of the sheds with sheets and decorated it with candles and flowers. Mr. Emerson and other friends joined the celebration and shared the refreshments: dried figs, nuts, and a birthday cake.

On Abbie May's second birthday, Uncle Junius (Bronson's younger brother) rowed the family down the Sudbury River. They picnicked on the bluffs above Walden Pond. Mrs. Alcott brought a cake, and the girls picked berries. The summer air was rich with the scents of pine forest and meadows. Spooning up her berries with milk and sugar, gazing out over the shining pond, Louy felt perfectly happy. She was even glad that Abbie May had been born.

All the months that Bronson Alcott was in England, he wrote long letters home. Mrs. Alcott read the letters out loud to Anna and Louy and Lizzie. Even little Abbie May sat quietly and listened as Marmee stroked her blond curls. Louy seemed to hear Papa's voice in the words, behind her mother's voice.

"I think of you all every day," he wrote. He described the way he thought of each of his four daughters. "Louisa, with her quick and ready senses, her agile limbs and boundless curiosity; her penetrating mind and tear-shedding heart . . ."

Sometimes Papa's words were like a brook, pleasant to listen to but hard to understand.

And then sometimes his words rang with a deep meaning that made Louy catch her breath. "A family is the heaven of the Soul."

Mrs. Alcott and the girls gathered from the letters that Mr. Alcott was spending a great deal of time talking with his new English friends. They talked about how to educate children, what people should eat, how people should live together. It was high-flown philosophical talk, but over the months the talk turned into plans.

Then Bronson Alcott wrote his family again, announcing that he was coming home. But not by himself. Two of the friends he had visited in England, Henry Wright and Charles Lane, as well as Mr. Lane's son William, were coming with him. They would all begin a new life together, in a new community. "The Newness" would be paradise on earth.

One day, when the maple trees in the woods were aflame with autumn colors,

Bronson Alcott and his English friends arrived in Concord. Abby Alcott and the girls had been in a whirl of excitement for days, cleaning the house and decorating it with greens. And now Mr. Alcott was really here. Not just his imagined voice in letters, but his real self hugging and kissing his girls over and over.

Louy was so excited she couldn't stand still. It was almost like being sick with a fever, this happiness. "Marmee"—she caught her mother's arm and whispered, while Papa was showing the two Englishmen and the English boy around Dove Cottage—"what makes me so happy?"

Mrs. Alcott didn't answer, except with a look that said she knew how Louy felt. It was nearly too much to stand, being this happy. Abby Alcott's face was glowing, and tears of joy sparkled in her eyes.

The English friends moved into Dove Cottage. Charles Lane took Bronson's study with the fireplace for his bedroom, while Mr. Wright took one of the cold upstairs bedrooms. The six Alcotts squeezed into the remaining bedroom and alcove. They began the way of life they called "the Newness."

As autumn turned into winter and they had to stay indoors, Dove Cottage seemed even more crowded. Louy began to notice that the main differences in the Alcotts' lives were unpleasant ones. The household ate their meals— unleavened bread, apples, and cold boiled potatoes—from napkins, because it was wasteful to wash needless dishes.

There was less food to go around, and Charles Lane frowned if Mrs. Alcott gave the children milk or sugar. Mr. Lane drew up a strict daily routine, beginning with cold baths. He taught the children their lessons in the morning.

Charles Lane and Bronson Alcott seemed to agree on ideas, and the words they spoke to the children were often the same. But the difference, Louy thought, was that Papa wanted them to be happy. Mr. Lane's thin lips, on the other hand, pressed together disapprovingly if the children enjoyed themselves too much.

Watching her mother, Louy saw the hurt look on her face as Mr. Lane frowned at her jokes. Again Louy began to hear her parents arguing late at night.

"How can you allow him to *reproach* me for my 'maternal love'?" Abby Alcott exclaimed. "Yes, I admit it—I am a mother. I admit it—I love my children!" Then Bronson's low voice, soothing, quietly reasoning.

Mrs. Alcott could not be soothed very long. The day before Christmas, she packed a bag for herself and Louy and young William Lane. "We need a rest from the Newness," she said crisply.

Louy didn't need an explanation for a trip to Boston. Visiting her aunts and uncles and cousins would have been a treat at any time, but especially after the last three months. In Boston, Louy whirled happily through parties and dinners and more parties in warm, brightly lighted rooms, with everyone laughing. There was a special trip to Amory Hall to see the candles lighted on the German Christmas tree. Even breakfasts were like parties. The aunts smiled approvingly as Louy poured cream and sprinkled sugar on her porridge.

But the best thing, for Louy, was to see her mother in high spirits once more. Louy was happy just to be with her.

Then Bronson wrote a letter begging his wife to come back, and Charles Lane came to Boston and made up with Abby Alcott. The whole family were reunited in Concord. The problem, the adults decided, was that they needed the right home for their community.

The "Consociate Family," as Bronson Alcott and Charles Lane called it, required roomier living quarters. And they needed a large farm to grow their own food and clothing: grain, vegetables, fruit, and flax for linen. All the better if the new home for the Consociate Family was far away from bad influences—the kind of influences that caused Henry Wright to desert his friends in January.

In the spring, they found a farm out in Harvard, Massachusetts, fourteen miles west of Concord. "Fruitlands," Mr. Alcott called it. Louy imagined rows of trees and vines, dripping with apples and pears and grapes.

On a clear, cold day at the beginning of June, the Consociate Family piled all their goods into a wagon. Serene-faced Bronson drove the horse, while young William Lane perched beside him holding the bust of Socrates. Abby rode in the back with three-year-old Abbie May on her lap, and Anna and Lizzie crouched under a shawl, playing with their dolls. Charles Lane, his face bony and humorless as usual, stalked in front of the wagon, his cloak billowing behind him. As for Louy, she tramped alongside the creaking wagon wheels.

The lurching, bumping journey over the hills took all day, but Louy and her sisters were still excited by the time the wagon left the road and inched up the last hill to a shabby red farmhouse. Abby Alcott looked tired, but her eyes shone with hope. The way Bronson Alcott had explained it—and he explained things so well—they would now be able to create their envisioned heaven on earth. The Newness would truly begin to work in their new home.

Hard Lessons

That first night, the travelers ate a quick supper of potatoes and bread and water and fell asleep on the floor. The next morning, they were rested enough to see what a beautiful place they had chosen for their New Eden. The farmhouse was set on the highest hill of ninety acres, looking west over pastures and wooded hills to Mount Wachusset. In the blue distance to the north rose the majestic peak of Mount Monadnock. The nearest house was out of sight, in a valley over a mile away.

"So this is Fruitlands," thought Louy. Her gaze shifted from the lofty view to the farm itself. She expected to see flourishing orchards and vineyards on every hill. But the only fruit-bearing plants in sight were ten scraggly apple trees that looked older than Grandfather May.

The house at Fruitlands was somewhat roomier than Dove Cottage, but dark and run-down. At first, it didn't seem to matter. As the men planted the crops, Mrs. Alcott and the girls set to work sweeping, scrubbing, whitewashing, and putting up curtains.

There was beautiful sunny weather all summer, and Anna and Louy and Lizzie spent their free time exploring the woods and meadows. The girls ran through the fields, pretending to be a herd of wild horses. They made paper gowns and wings for themselves, and took them into the woods and pretended to fly like fairies.

The Consociate Family at Fruitlands all wore linen clothes. Cotton was forbidden, since it was grown in the South with slave labor. Wool was forbidden, since it was taken from sheep by force. But linen came from the flax plant, which they could grow themselves. Louy liked her loose linen tunic, so comfortable in the summer heat.

Now Anna and Louy kept journals, as Mr. and Mrs. Alcott did. The parents encouraged their daughters to write down what happened each day, and what they thought about it. The journals weren't private—part of the idea was for the girls to share them with their parents and discuss how they were getting along.

On September 1, Louy wrote: "I rose at five and had my bath. I love cold water! Then we had our singing lesson with Mr. Lane. After breakfast I washed dishes, and ran up on the hill till nine, and had some thoughts— it was so beautiful up there."

At nine the girls had lessons in writing and spelling and arithmetic with Charles Lane.

Later in the morning, Bronson Alcott talked with the girls, encouraging them to think about deep questions. "What is God's noblest work?" he asked. Anna thought the right answer was "men."

"Babies," said Louy, without hesitating. "Men are often bad; babies never are."

In her diary Louy went on to record the midday dinner of bread and fruit. That afternoon she spent reading and walking and playing. After supper, Mr. Lane played his violin while the family sang.

The moon was full that night, and Louy saw it from her bedroom window as she put on her nightgown. It seemed to be a face looking at her. "Well, Louisa?" it asked silently. "Were you good today?" Louy thought of all the times she had been cross with her sisters or hadn't minded her mother. She burst into tears.

After crying, Louy felt better. Climbing into bed beside Anna, she pulled the covers

up around her chin and began to recite a poem to herself. She was asleep before she had finished.

No matter how bad Louy felt about herself, she always felt better for writing in her journal. It was like a letter to her mother. She knew that Marmee would read it and understand how she felt. Sometimes her mother would write an answer in her journal. These days, when Louy watched blond, blue-eyed little Abbie May sitting on her mother's lap, she didn't feel quite so jealous. Her youngest sister couldn't share her thoughts with their mother the way Louisa did.

One of the naughty things Louy did (but she never cried over this) was to tease Charles Lane. She knew she ought to be respectful and grateful to Mr. Lane. After all, he was the one (along with Uncle Sam May) who had paid for their new home. Mr. Lane was an educated man, and he spent hours teaching the Alcott children. He worked hard at trying to make them better people.

But it was so easy to tease Mr. Lane and get away with it! He never understood a joke. Once in a while he smiled, but never because he thought something was funny.

During lessons one morning, Mr. Lane had Louy and Anna and Lizzie write a list of their faults. The idea was to think about their bad points so they could try to improve. Louy scribbled her long list quickly, all the faults that made her cry at bedtime: temper, willfulness, vanity, idleness, impudence . . .

Glancing up from her paper, she noticed the big gray cat by the schoolroom door. He sat in the middle of a patch of sunlight, eyes half closed. The cat wasn't thinking about how to improve himself; he was just soaking up the warmth. Impulsively, Louy ended her list of faults with: love of cats.

When Louy read her list out loud, she kept a straight face. But she saw Anna bite her lip to keep from smiling. Lizzie gave a surprised giggle. Mr. Lane looked sternly first at Lizzie, then at the cat.

"He truly believes my love of cats *is* a fault," thought Louy. In the Consociate Family, they were all supposed to love each other. But it was hard to like Mr. Lane.

There was an enormous amount of work to be done on the farm, and it was already late in the season. At first the men worked hard at plowing the rocky soil and planting the crops for their strict diet. Many visitors came to Fruitlands to see firsthand this heaven on earth of plain living and universal love. Some of the visitors joined the Consociate Family for a time and helped with the work. Ralph Emerson came on July 4, looking rather lonely for his friends, but he didn't stay.

Toward the end of the summer, Bronson Alcott began taking frequent trips to Boston. Charles Lane became restless, too, and they both left on a long lecture tour. They explained their philosophy to audiences in Rhode Island, New York, Connecticut, and New Hampshire.

Meanwhile, the barley crop was ripe. When an easterly storm threatened to ruin the grain, Mrs. Alcott led the girls and William Lane into the fields with baskets and bedsheets. One woman and four children saved the Consociate Family's food for the winter.

Again the trees turned brilliant orange and red and yellow. Out here in the country, against the backdrop of the mountains, autumn was even more beautiful than in Concord. On October 8, Louy woke up thinking, "It's Mother's birthday. I must be very good."

At breakfast Louy gave her mother her presents: a cross made of velvety green moss and a poem she had written. On this special day there was no school, and the girls played in the woods and picked red leaves to decorate the house. That evening, Charles Lane played his violin while the family danced and sang.

At the end of the day, though, Louy felt let down. She wrote in her diary: "I wish I was rich, I was good, and we were all a happy family this day."

The problems with the Fruitlands community began to add up. With a chill in the air, the rules about cold baths and linen clothes were not so pleasant. The crops had not done as well as Bronson had hoped. There was still a great deal of work to be done, but all the men except Mr. Alcott and Mr. Lane had left the community. Abby Alcott and Charles Lane hardly spoke to each other.

Once when Louy was helping her mother in the kitchen, her father came in with an armful of kindling. He set down the wood by the fireplace, then came up behind Abby

Alcott and dropped a kiss on the top of her thick, shiny hair.

Watching her parents, Louy felt warm and happy. But then she glanced up and caught sight of Mr. Lane in the doorway. He was watching her mother and father, too, and he did not look warm and happy.

"Why—he's jealous," thought Louy in astonishment. "He's just as jealous of Marmee as I am of Abbie May!"

The cold weather began early that year. A week before Louy's eleventh birthday, the food and firewood at Fruitlands were almost gone. Worse, there was none at all of the "universal love" that was supposed to blossom in the Consociate Family. Charles Lane felt the problem was the close family ties among the Alcotts—that their special love for each other stood in the way of the "community of universal love" that he and Bronson Alcott had set out to build.

One evening Charles Lane and Bronson

Alcott had a long talk in the study. The three older girls and Mrs. Alcott sat in the living room, sewing. Louy bent over the cape she was making for her doll, trying to keep her mind off the men's voices rising and falling in the next room.

The next day Charles Lane trudged off through drifts of snow, toward Concord, to think things over. But the struggle was not over. Bronson and Abby Alcott brought Louy and Anna into the decision making, telling them frankly that the Consociate Family was breaking up. Mrs. Alcott and Mr. Lane were not willing to live with each other anymore.

The parents and the two older girls talked it over. Their father seemed to hope that Louy or Anna might persuade their mother to give the Consociate Family one more chance. Bronson could hardly bear to think of giving up his vision of the ideal community. But Louy said, "I like Fruitlands, but not the school part or Mr. Lane."

Days and weeks passed, while the Alcotts discussed and cried. Louy and Anna were miserable. Their father was seriously thinking of leaving them.

On December 10, Louy wrote in her diary: "I did my lessons, and walked in the afternoon. Father read to us in dear *Pilgrim's Progress*. Mr. Lane was in Boston, and we were glad. In the eve Father and Mother and Anna and I had a long talk. I was very unhappy, and we all cried. Anna and I cried in bed, and I prayed God to keep us all together."

By Christmas Eve, Charles Lane had returned to Fruitlands. This year, it was Bronson Alcott, rather than Abby, who left for Boston by himself. Anna, Louy, Lizzie, and Abbie May opened their stockings on Christmas morning without him. Abby sang and played with her girls, while yet another snowstorm howled outside.

Bronson didn't come back home until New Year's Day. A few days later, Charles Lane and his son William left Fruitlands for good. Bronson fell into a deep depression, and lay in bed for several days without eating. Listening outside their parents' bedroom, Louy and Anna heard their mother crying and pleading, but they didn't hear their father speak.

Then, one day in January, Bronson Alcott appeared leaning on Abby's arm, very pale and thin, but trying to smile at his daughters. "My faithful wife—my little girls," he murmured. A few days later, the Alcotts loaded their few belongings onto a neighbor's ox sled and left the New Eden.

Back to Concord

Leaving Fruitlands in January 1844, the Alcotts stayed with neighbors until they could rent half a house in nearby Still River. After months of being taught by Mr. Lane, Louy and Anna and Lizzie were overjoyed to go to a regular school. The nice young teacher, Miss Chase, never asked them to list their faults.

The Alcott girls also loved being with other children again, and they quickly made friends. As usual, Louy was the leader in the games. Besides the races and tree climbing, they played many pretend games. Once Louy draped a white apron over her head for a bridal veil and acted out marrying a boy named Walter Gardener. The woodshed made a good church, and another boy played the minister. The "marriage" broke down soon after the ceremony, as Louy and Walter quarreled and slapped each other.

In June the Alcotts celebrated Lizzie's ninth birthday in the old joyous style. They decorated the house with greens and invited all the neighbor children to a feast of cherries and cake. Timid, gentle Lizzie, embarrassed to be the center of attention, gladly let Louy and Anna entertain the guests. Anna, dressed like a Scottish Highlander in a flat cap and plaid, recited a ballad about Scotland. Louy, with her skin stained reddish brown, costumed like an Indian maiden, sang songs and recited poetry in a dramatic style.

That fall, the Alcotts decided to return to Concord. They would board with the

Hosmers, because Bronson Alcott was unemployed, and they had no money to rent a house of their own. Abby Alcott still hoped to receive her small inheritance from her father's will, although it had now been three years since Colonel May's death. On the other hand, Mr. Alcott's Boston creditors were still trying to claim that money to repay his debts.

On this trip, the Alcotts rode the new railroad train from Littleton to Concord. Gazing out the window at the November landscape flashing past, Louy remembered the plodding day-long trip in the wagon from Concord to Fruitlands. She looked across the aisle at her mother and father, and noticed that her father's blond hair had turned gray. His shoulders were stooped, as if to show he had given up his dream of a splendid new society.

Abby Alcott, though, had *not* given up. Her mouth was set in a determined line, and her dark eyes were as sharp as ever. Louy knew that her mother had high hopes for her girls, and she would do everything in her power to make them come true.

Abbie May, the fourth and youngest Alcott sister, perched on the seat between her parents. At four years old, Abbie May seemed perfectly satisfied with herself. And why shouldn't she be? People were always telling her how pretty she was and giving her treats.

Louy glanced at her sister Anna beside her on the bench, her hands folded in her lap. With her sweet, ladylike manners, Anna seemed the opposite of tomboy Louy. But Anna showed another side when they put on their plays. She entered into the drama with just as much spirit as Louy did. After all their quarrels, the two sisters had become close friends.

Lizzie, on the other side of Anna, had her usual quiet, gentle look. Her hair was light brown, her cheeks very pink. Louy felt especially protective of Lizzie, who was shy with people outside her family.

As for Louy herself, she was tall like her mother, and like her mother she had thick, shiny hair. She didn't like to fuss with it, unless she was dressing up for a part in one of her plays. Louy's arms and legs had grown long, and it seemed she was always letting down the hems of her skirts. Her feet, sticking out into the aisle in her worn laced boots, looked too big on her thin legs. She felt different, quite different from the girl of eleven who had followed the creaking wagon out to Fruitlands.

As the Alcotts settled back into Concord, Louy began to look at her family and the people of Concord with a new awareness. Her mother, she could see, was ashamed to return to Concord after their failure at Fruitlands. People thought the Alcotts were peculiar. They laughed at Bronson Alcott, the grand philosopher who couldn't seem to make a living for his family. Mr. Alcott had hoped to set up a new school in Concord with Miss Sophia Foord as his assistant, but no one would lend him money for it.

At least the Emersons, the Hosmers, and Henry Thoreau were the Alcotts' steadfast friends. True, Henry was just as odd as the Alcotts, in the opinion of Concord. He was determined to build a cabin in the woods on Walden Pond and live there all by himself. Bronson, who was as fond of Henry as if he had been his son, helped him put the roof on the cabin.

Sophia Foord was a great admirer of Bronson Alcott's ideas, and she stayed with the Alcotts for a time. She gave the girls book lessons, and she also took them out in nature to teach them about plants. Louy and her sisters especially loved the time Miss Foord led them splashing all the way across Finch Pond. They returned home "all wet and muddy," Louy wrote a friend in Still River, "but we were happy enough, for we came through the woods bawling and singing like crazy folks." After Louy fell out of an apple tree, Miss Foord gave the girls a lesson on the bones of the human body.

Louy was troubled by her moods, which seemed to go up and down more than ever these days. Like her mother, she had a temper that could flare up suddenly. One day in January 1845, she wrote in her diary: "I got angry and called Anna mean. Father told me to look [up] the word in the Dic.[tionary], and it meant 'base,' 'contemptible.' I was so ashamed to have called my dear sister that, and I cried over my bad tongue and temper."

The Concord folk thought Louy was odd for climbing and jumping and running, when she should be learning to walk like a young lady. But she could run faster than any boy in town, Louy thought with satisfaction. Besides, the way she felt when she ran was more important to her than the neighbors' *tsk tsks.*

"I had an early run in the woods before the dew was off the grass," she wrote in her diary one autumn day. "The moss was like velvet, and as I ran under the arches of red and yellow leaves I sang for joy, my heart was so bright and the world so beautiful. . . .

"A very strange and solemn feeling came over me as I stood there, with no sound but the rustle of the pines, no one near me, and the sun so glorious, as for me alone. It seemed as if I *felt* God as I never did before, and I prayed in my heart that I might keep that happy sense of nearness all my life."

By the spring of 1845, Abby Alcott had finally received her inheritance from her father's will. It was enough to buy a house. After all these years of moving from one rental to the next or living with friends, the Alcotts would have a house of their own.

Ralph Emerson found one just right for them, on the Lexington road a short walk from the Emersons. Bronson named it "Hillside," because it was set on the slope of a ridge.

The family moved into their new home on April 1, 1845. It still wasn't big enough for the six Alcotts, and warm-hearted Mrs. Alcott also took in an orphan boy, Llewellyn Willis, to spend the summer. Louy and Anna and Lizzie and little Abbie May had to share the upstairs bedroom. But Bronson Alcott was a good carpenter, and he was happy to set to work rebuilding the house.

There was a workshop on the property, because the former owner had been a wheelwright. Cutting the shop in two, Mr. Alcott added one half to each side of the house to form wings. He also rigged up a bathhouse for cold shower-baths and moved the barn from the farmland across the road.

Llewellyn became good friends with the

Alcott girls, especially tomboy Louy. He joined the Alcotts on picnics, berry-picking expeditions, and walks in the woods. One of the sisters' special amusements was their "post office," a hollow stump they had found on the hill in back of their house, where they exchanged letters with their Concord friends.

The children spent many hours with Henry Thoreau. Henry could whistle in a low, odd way that made woodchucks, squirrels, and crows come right up to him. He rowed the children out on Walden Pond, sometimes letting the boat drift while he played the flute.

Louy was delighted to be back in Concord and in their own house at last. Still, there was one more thing she longed for. She wrote her mother a letter about it:

"Dearest Mother

I have tryed to be more contented and I think I have been more so. I have been

thinking about my little room which I sup-
pose I shall never have. I should want to be
there all the time and I should go there and
sing and think."

She ended the letter: "From your trying
daughter, Louy."

Louy loved that kind of word play. She was
trying "to be more contented." At the same
time, she knew she had often *tried* her parents' patience, ever since she was a little
child.

All the Alcott children had been brought
up to think of other people first, and not to
complain about doing without. Louy would
never have asked for a room of her own, if it
hadn't been something she really needed.

Louisa's Room

It was March 1846. Louisa was thirteen and a half—and she was standing in the middle of *her own room*. It was on the first floor, with a door into the garden. She could dash straight outside, and run and run, whenever she got into one of her wild moods.

Her own room, at last! Louisa poked her head into the closet and sniffed the sweet-smelling herbs her mother had hung there. With a sigh of happiness, she sat down at her desk by the window and picked up a pen.

"I have made a plan for my life," she wrote

in her diary, "as I am in my teens, and no more a child. I am old for my age, and don't care much for girls' things. . . . Now I'm going to *work really*, for I feel a true desire to improve, and be a help and comfort, not a care and sorrow, to my dear mother."

On November 29, Louisa's fourteenth birthday, Abby Alcott gave Louisa a new pen. It was a token of the great hopes she had for her second daughter's career as a writer. Mrs. Alcott had composed a poem to go with the present. "Oh, may this pen your muse inspire," it began.

Louisa had great hopes for herself, too. She wrote constantly: poems, songs, plays. The plays were highly unrealistic dramas, involving murder, magic potions, and high-flown declarations of love. They were set in exotic places Louisa had never seen, such as Spain or Greece.

But one feature of the plays was Louisa's own. The women in her melodramas were not typical nineteenth-century heroines, waiting around to be rescued or victimized by men. They were strong, passionate women who could perform their own heroic feats.

The play Louisa was proudest of was a four-act melodrama: *Norna, or The Witch's Curse.* It featured Count Rudolph (played by Louisa); a gallant hero (Louisa), the witch Norna (Anna), Count Rudolph's murdered wife, Theresa (Anna), assassins, courtiers, and many more.

As soon as Bronson moved the barn across the road, the Alcott sisters claimed it as their theater. By now Anna and Louisa and Lizzie were all skilled seamstresses, and they made their own costumes from old sheets, curtains, and shawls. Bits of tin became spangles for an elegant gown, or links in a soldier's armor. They constructed elaborate sets, piling up furniture to create a luxurious palace, or a cave in a gloomy wood.

Neighborhood children, including the

Hosmers and the Emersons, were the audience, and Mrs. Alcott often left her work to attend performances. Part of the fun for Louisa and Anna, playing all the main roles, was changing in seconds from a lovely heroine to a hideous witch, or from a noble courtier to a pirate. Louisa especially loved stomping around the "stage" in a pair of secondhand boots that a family friend had given her.

Another favorite pastime of Louisa's was reading. She loved Charles Dickens for his humorous characters and his dramatic plots. She and her family read *Oliver Twist, The Pickwick Papers,* and *Martin Chuzzlewit* over and over, as well as Sir Walter Scott's historical novels, such as *Ivanhoe*. Often one of the Alcott girls would read aloud while the others sewed.

Like many teenage girls, Louisa longed for romance. She wasn't interested in the boys of Concord—she wanted to love someone noble and good, a creative genius. There actually was such an ideal man in Concord: Ralph Emerson. Of course he was old enough to be her father, and already married, with children. But Louisa liked yearning over a hero who would be forever out of reach.

Louisa knew firsthand what a good person Mr. Emerson was, for he was the best friend the Alcotts had. In many ways, he was like her father. Ralph Waldo Emerson was tall and lean, with intensely blue eyes and a serene manner. He was a philosopher, like Bronson Alcott.

But unlike Bronson, Ralph Emerson never seemed to have money troubles. In fact, it was his money that often bailed the Alcotts out of dire poverty. He had paid the extra five hundred dollars so that they could buy Hillside. Sometimes, after he had visited the Alcotts, they would find money slipped tactfully behind a jar on the mantel, or tucked under a book.

Ralph Emerson welcomed Louisa to his

study, a quiet, book-lined room with a round mahogany writing table. He made suggestions about what she might like to read next, let her borrow from his library, and discussed the books with her when she brought them back. Here on his bookshelves she found Shakespeare's plays, the Italian poet Dante's works, and the great German writer Goethe's plays and poems.

A particularly thrilling book Louisa discovered in Mr. Emerson's library was an account of Goethe's friendship with a young girl, Bettine. In her imagination, she was Bettine and Mr. Emerson was Goethe. Thinking of Ralph Emerson's long, quiet face, and the way it lit up with a smile, Louisa wrote passionate letters telling him how she felt.

Louisa never sent those letters, of course. But sometimes she left bunches of wildflowers on Mr. Emerson's doorstep. Sometimes she sneaked out of her house late on a moonlit night and crept down the road and into the

Emersons' garden. She knew which room her hero was sleeping in, and she was satisfied with just looking up at his window.

The Emersons, the Alcotts, Henry Thoreau and his relatives, and many others in Concord were involved in the growing movement against slavery. In July 1846, Henry Thoreau had deliberately gone to jail rather than pay taxes to the United States government, which allowed slavery in the Southern states. Ralph Emerson disapproved of Henry's way of protesting slavery, while Bronson Alcott heartily applauded it. But about slavery itself, they completely agreed: It was evil; it must be destroyed.

The Alcotts and their Concord friends took part in the Underground Railroad, an informal network of hiding places for slaves fleeing the South for Canada and freedom. In February 1847, the Alcotts took in a fugitive slave. Louisa, with the rest of the family, sat

by the fire and listened to this man tell of his life as a slave in Maryland. She watched him saw wood, and thought how glad he must be to give his labor to friends, instead of being forced to work like an ox or mule.

The Alcotts' ideals might be high, but they were sliding into debt again. Bronson had turned the neglected grounds of Hillside into a beautiful garden, and he had made their fields across the road produce a bounty of vegetables and fruit. But although they owned their house, the Alcotts had no money to keep it up. And there was no money for the rest of their food or for clothes or for firewood, let alone the girls' education.

Now that she was "no longer a child," Louisa was eager to begin earning money. She longed to be independent, and she longed to help her family, especially her mother. She began a little school for the young Emerson children, teaching them reading and arithmetic. She also told them stories. Louisa's favorite was Ellen Emerson, who especially loved the stories Louisa made up about fairies. Louisa wrote the stories out in booklets and gave them to Ellen.

In spite of Louisa's efforts, the Alcotts could not make ends meet. One gloomy November afternoon in 1847, the Alcotts held a family council. They couldn't go on living this way, but Bronson and Abby Alcott couldn't agree about what to do. They thought of selling the house, but no one wanted to buy it.

Mr. and Mrs. Alcott argued all through the winter of 1847–48. Abby tried to persuade her husband to go to Maine, where they had been offered jobs and a free cottage at a mountain resort. By springtime, she was desperate. Taking seven-year-old Abbie May, she left to work in Maine on her own.

Anna began to earn money, too. Visiting a cousin in Walpole, New Hampshire, she found a teaching job and stayed on through the summer. In the fall, she went to work as a governess in a family in Jamaica Plain, near Boston.

For Louisa, the summer of 1848 was an anxious and lonely time. She missed Anna and her mother terribly, and she wondered what would become of the Alcotts. But at the end of the summer, Mrs. Alcott returned. She couldn't bear living without her family. At the same time, she was more determined than ever to earn money.

That autumn, everything seemed to fall into place. Friends of Abby Alcott's in Boston arranged to hire her as a charity worker, visiting the poor of the city. Bronson Alcott, too, was now earning some money by holding "conversations" or discussion groups and giving lectures in Boston. And just in time, a tenant turned up to rent Hillside.

So on November 17, a bitterly cold day, the Alcotts moved once more. They rode from Concord into the city on the new train. They would live in the basement rooms of a house on Dedham Street, in the South End. While Mrs. Alcott went out to work full time, Lizzie and Abbie May would go to school. And Louisa, now almost sixteen, would keep house for the family.

Earning a Living

Cooking and cleaning the house was not Louisa's goal in life, but for now it was the best she could do to help the family. She worked at housekeeping as energetically as her mother always had. She made up a song to sing loudly while she did the laundry:

Queen of my tub, I merrily sing
While the white foam rises high,
And sturdily wash, and rinse, and wring,
And fasten the clothes to dry . . .

Louisa was proud of her mother, earning money for the family and at the same time helping people much needier than the Alcotts. Boston at this time was crowded with immigrants from Germany and Ireland, as well as free blacks. The Irish were mostly uneducated, unskilled, and desperately poor. They lived in slums, sometimes fourteen to one small room. Abby Alcott distributed food and clothing and medicine, found jobs for the unemployed, and walked miles every day visiting her clients.

In July 1848, the first women's rights convention had been held at Seneca Falls, New York. Elizabeth Cady Stanton, Lucretia Mott, and other leaders asserted that women ought to be able to vote and to own property after marriage. Abby Alcott knew from her personal experience, and from working in the slums, how important it was for women to gain these rights. She began speaking out in public on women's issues. She also organized a petition, presented to the Massachusetts State Constitutional Convention, for women's right to vote.

The Alcotts might be poor, but they had each other. The girls now put on their plays for the Boston cousins in their kitchen, dubbed the "Olympia Theater." They were more skillful than ever at creating sets and costumes. "We make harps, castles, armor, dresses, waterfalls, and thunder, and have great fun," Louisa wrote in her diary.

In honor of their favorite author, Charles Dickens, and his novel *The Pickwick Papers*, the girls formed their own "Pickwick Club." At the meetings they read aloud a newspaper written entirely by the four of them: poems, stories, reports, recipes, advice.

In one issue Anna, always ladylike, contributed a piece about the importance of keeping the fingernails clean. Louisa had written a long poem to her cat, "To Pat Paws," beginning:

Oh my kitty Oh my darling
Purring softly on my knee

While your sleepy little eyes dear
Look so fondly up at me

Lizzie contributed an essay on botany, while Abbie May had written a report titled "A Trip to Nahant." There were also many more stories, poems, and columns, including an entertainment section announcing the opening of the "Olympia Theater."

In January 1850, Louisa began to help Anna run her little school. Lizzie, so shy that she had been unhappy at school, took over keeping house. Louisa was eager to earn money for the family, but she didn't have as much patience for teaching as Anna. "School is hard work," wrote Louisa in her diary, "and I feel as though I should like to run away from it."

These days, Louisa badly missed the Concord countryside. "Among my hills and woods I had fine free times alone," she wrote, "and though my thoughts were silly, I

116

daresay, they helped to keep me happy and good."

Dissatisfied with herself, Louisa listed her struggles in her diary that May: "If I look in my glass, I try to keep down vanity about my long hair, my well-shaped head, and my good nose. In the street I try not to covet fine things. My quick tongue is always getting me into trouble, and my moodiness makes it hard to be cheerful when I think how poor we are, how much worry it is to live, and how many things I long to do I never can."

Louisa also missed the times when her mother used to read her diary and write encouraging notes in it. "I can't talk to anyone but Mother about my troubles, and she has so many now to bear I try not to add any more."

That same year, 1850, Congress passed the Fugitive Slave Act, bitterly nicknamed the "Bloodhound Bill." This law stated that black slaves could not escape their masters by running away to the North, where slavery was outlawed. Slave catchers could hunt them down even in Boston. Anyone helping a slave to escape could be fined or thrown in jail. The Alcotts heartily agreed with Ralph Emerson, who called the law "a filthy enactment. . . . I will not obey it, by God."

After two years of social work, Abby Alcott realized that the poor Irish immigrants she visited needed jobs more than anything else. Giving up charity work, she opened an employment office in her home. She matched workers—cooks, maids, seamstresses—with employers.

Louisa, now eighteen, sometimes helped her mother in the office. She happened to be there one day in 1851 when a promising job came up. A Mr. Richardson, a gentleman from Dedham (near Boston) wanted to hire a live-in companion for his invalid sister. The companion would be asked to do a little light housework, he said. But she would be treated as one of the family, with the use of their library and piano.

"Why couldn't I go, Mother?" exclaimed Louisa. This job would be more interesting than teaching or sewing, she thought. She would have the advantages of living in a cultured home. And it was a chance for her to be independent.

But after a short time in Dedham, she realized that the "gentleman" had other ideas about Louisa's role in the house. Mr. Richardson tried to start long, private conversations with her. He hung around and made eyes at her when she was trying to dust or scrub. He wrote her suggestive notes and slipped them under her bedroom door. Disgusted, Louisa finally told him to leave her alone.

From that moment, Mr. Richardson dumped the hardest work in the household on her. She had to haul water, shovel snow, split kindling. Now she was not even a lady's companion—she was a household drudge.

After almost two months of this mistreatment, Louisa quit. It had been unpleasant, thankless work. But at least, she thought, she was taking home real money to her family. As she said good-bye to the timid invalid sister, the woman had tucked a little purse into Louisa's hand.

Carrying her luggage to the Dedham train station, Louisa stopped in the road to find out just how much money she was taking home. To her shock, the purse contained only four dollars. Even in 1851, that was not fair pay for seven weeks' hard labor. Louisa's only comfort was her family's indignation. Mr. and Mrs. Alcott sent back the insulting four dollars.

Although the Alcotts were struggling themselves, they were always taking in strays. "Our poor little home . . . was a shelter for lost girls, abused wives, friendless children, and weak or wicked men," wrote Louisa.

Some friends and relatives criticized the Alcotts for exposing their daughters to what they thought were bad influences. But to Louisa, her parents' generosity was a lesson in "practical Christianity."

Louisa herself worked on, teaching and sewing. Sewing was in some ways more pleasant, because she could make up stories and poems and plays as she worked. In her spare time, she wrote and wrote. She even wrote a romantic novel, *The Inheritance*.

In September 1851, Louisa saw her writing in print for the first time. Her poem "Sunlight" was published in *Peterson's Magazine*. The next spring, her story "The Rival Painters," written when she was sixteen, was published. Llewellen Willis, the boy whom the Alcotts had befriended in Concord, had taken the story to the editor of the *Olive Branch*.

Proudly Louisa gazed at her words in print. And the *Olive Branch* had paid her five dollars! Maybe some day she could actually make a living by writing.

The Alcotts weren't quite as desperately poor now, because their house "Hillside" in Concord was finally sold. The buyer was Nathaniel Hawthorne, the eccentric author of *The Scarlet Letter* and *The House of the Seven Gables.* The Alcotts moved to a house on Pinckney Street on Beacon Hill, a more pleasant section of Boston. There Anna and Louisa ran a school for young children in the parlor.

The following year Anna left for Syracuse, where Uncle Sam May now lived, to teach in a school there. Louisa, still running the school in their parlor, missed her older sister badly. Anna was the only one with whom she could discuss the family problems. "Dear Nan," wrote Louisa in the spring of 1854. "I am grubbing away, trying to get enough money to buy Mother a nice warm shawl."

Louisa also had schemes to help her sister

Abbie May. She wanted to dress her in "silk and lace" and have her enjoy "bottles of cream" and trips to Europe. For now, Louisa put together a fetching bonnet for her pretty younger sister, using her old straw bonnet, odds and ends from her scrap bag, and a new crimson ribbon.

Louisa was also thinking of Lizzie, who always had to wear Anna and Louisa's hand-me-downs. Lizzie would have a new dress, Louisa planned. And she could make her father happy, she knew, with some neckties and writing paper.

Meanwhile, Bronson Alcott was earning a *little* money by holding his "Conversations." He lectured to small groups on such philosophical topics as "The Mysteries of Life." In the fall of 1853, he set out on a tour of upstate New York and Ohio. Ralph Emerson paid Bronson's train fare.

In Cincinnati, people were so enthusiastic about this philosopher-poet from the cultured East Coast that he earned $150. He promptly sent the money home, with a proud letter. At last, it seemed, he had found the way to make good money and still respect himself.

Late one cold, wet February night, Bronson Alcott returned from his tour and arrived home at the house in Pinckney Street. Abby Alcott and the girls ran downstairs in their nightgowns to welcome him and fuss over him. Of course the girls were delighted to have their father safe home, but they were all thinking the same thing: Did he make any more money?

Finally Abbie May asked the question out loud. With a sad smile, Mr. Alcott opened his wallet and showed them one dollar. Many people had promised to pay him, he said, but they had not paid. Someone had stolen his overcoat. "Another year I shall do better."

Louisa looked from her thin, tired father,

dirty from travel, to her mother in a nightcap and an old jacket thrown over her nightgown. She saw the love on her mother's face as she kissed Bronson and said tenderly, "I call that doing *very well*." And Louisa never forgot the answering love on her father's weary face.

Louisa hadn't quite put aside her miserable experience working for the "gentleman" in Dedham. She was beginning to realize that the worst troubles make the best stories, and she thought she might earn some money from this one at last. After writing up the experience as a story, she took the manuscript to the Old Corner Bookstore on Washington Street. There Mr. James T. Fields, a book publisher, had his office in a back room.

Louisa sat nervously while Mr. Fields flipped the pages, saying nothing. Finally he looked up and smiled. Louisa's heart beat hopefully.

"Stick to your teaching, Miss Alcott," said the publisher. "You can't write."

Mr. Fields's words hurt, but Louisa had no intention of taking his advice. She would keep on writing. Some day, she would prove him wrong.

Author Louisa

In May 1854, Boston was in a turmoil. The Fugitive Slave Law, that "filthy enactment" as Ralph Emerson called it, was being enforced on the streets of the Alcotts' city. Anthony Burns, a runaway slave from Virginia, had been kidnapped by Federal marshals and imprisoned in the Boston courthouse. If the law had its way, Anthony Burns would be returned to his owner.

Bronson Alcott was a member of the abolitionist Committee of Vigilance, led by the Unitarian preacher Theodore Parker. The committee had already broken the law twice, trying to rescue captured runaway slaves. Now this group, including Bronson, stormed the Boston courthouse and tried to rescue Anthony Burns. They failed, and some of the would-be rescuers were arrested or injured.

On June 2, when army guards marched Anthony Burns in shackles from the courthouse to the waterfront, Boston was draped in black for the tragedy. From house after house, the Stars and Stripes hung upside down. The Alcotts and thousands of others crowded the streets, shouting, "Kidnappers! Shame!" Louisa caught sight of Burns, a young man about her age—but with what a different history. Gazing at his scarred face, she vowed to do *something* to help free the slaves.

When she was not teaching her little school in the Pinckney Street parlor or sewing for money, Louisa climbed up to the privacy of her garret room and wrote. In November, she received the best birthday present a writer could wish for. "The Rival Prima Donnas," her story of jealousy, murder, insanity, and general melodrama, was published in the *Saturday Evening Gazette*. She was paid ten dollars.

That winter, Louisa's first book was published, earning her the glory of authorship and thirty-two dollars besides. The book was *Flower Fables*, a collection of the stories Louisa had written several years ago for Ellen Emerson. She dedicated the book to Ellen, and sent her a copy. But most of all she wanted to share her triumph with her mother, who had always encouraged her and believed in her.

"Dear Mother," wrote Louisa in a note tucked into *Flower Fables*, "Into your Christmas stocking I have put my 'first-born' . . . Whatever beauty or poetry is to be found in my little book is owing to your interest in and encouragement of all my efforts from the first to the last . . . "

Fittingly, Abby Alcott gave Louisa a writing desk that Christmas. Abby was feeling old and weary and discouraged these days. She was ready to give up the struggle to earn a living and make a difference in the world. But she still had great hopes for Louisa.

In the summer the Alcotts decided to move to Walpole, New Hampshire, a resort town up in the hills. They were short of money, as usual, and Abby's brother-in-law, Uncle Benjamin Willis, had offered them the use of a rent-free house there. Once in Walpole, Louisa fell into a pleasant routine of early-morning runs through the woods, then writing, then driving in the afternoon, then fun in the evening.

Louisa and Anna and Abbie May enthusiastically joined the other young people of Walpole in summer theatricals. Abbie May worked as the prompter, while Anna and Louisa acted. Louisa was a resounding success in comic parts such as Mrs. Malaprop in *The Rivals*.

That fall Bronson and Abby stayed in New Hampshire, while Anna reluctantly returned to Syracuse to teach. Louisa packed her trunk for Boston, determined to seek her fortune as a writer. Having only twenty dollars, she had to live with relatives and friends.

November 29, Louisa and Bronson's mutual birthday (her twenty-third and his fifty-sixth), came around again. The day before, she sent her father a letter. "I think it is but right & proper that a thanksgiving feast should be held in the states where we both are, to celebrate the joyful day on which two such blessings as you & I dawned upon the world," she wrote teasingly. She imagined how different the two of them were as babies: "I know *you* were a serene & placid baby when you began your wise meditations in the quiet little Spindle Hill farm house . . . *I* was a crass crying brown baby, bawling at the disagreeable old world where on a dismal November day I found myself, & began my long fight . . ."

Louisa earned money by sewing, as usual, but she was also writing as hard as she could. Scrimping on herself, she managed to send her family in New Hampshire a box of Christmas presents to "cheer the dear souls in the snowbanks." She sold one story after another.

Readers of the *Saturday Evening Gazette* began to notice how entertaining the stories by "L.M.A." were, and to ask for more. In January 1856, the *Gazette* advertised her story "Bertha" as a major attraction. "Got $10 for 'Bertha,'" she wrote gleefully in her diary, "and saw great yellow placards stuck up announcing it."

In June, Louisa returned to Walpole, New Hampshire, for another season of fresh air and theater productions. But this summer was not a carefree one like the last. Tender-hearted Abby Alcott had nursed a neighbor's sick children and brought home scarlet fever. When Louisa arrived in Walpole, she found Lizzie and May sick with this serious disease. Lizzie was *very* ill.

"An anxious time," Louisa noted in her diary. She spent the summer nursing her sisters and keeping house, although she managed to write a few stories in between.

In the fall Mr. and Mrs. Alcott stayed on in Walpole again. Louisa moved back to Boston, more determined than ever to seek her fortune. "I was born with a boy's spirit under my bib and tucker," she told her diary. "I *can't wait* when I *can work*, so I took my little talent in hand and forced the world again . . ."

Louisa found an attic room at Mrs. Reed's boardinghouse on Chauncy Street, downtown. The rent, three dollars a week, included meals and a fire in her room. As for her clothes, she playfully wrote her sister Anna, they would "rain down from heaven, or the fashions . . . change to one comforter and a pair of boots." Louisa spent the mornings writing in her "sky-parlor," as she called the little room with a view of the blue sky and a gray church steeple.

For reliable income, Louisa got a job teaching a few hours a week. She also sewed—sheets, pillowcases, towels, dress-making—while she dreamed up stories. "I can sew like a steam engine while I plan my works of art," she wrote Anna. Louisa wasn't yet able to make a living from writing, but she was selling more and more of her stories. Mr. Clapp, the editor at the *Saturday Evening Gazette*, engaged her to write a story a month, for ten dollars a story.

Soon after her return to Boston, Louisa attended a welcoming ceremony at the State House for Senator Charles Sumner, an out-spoken champion for the abolition of slavery.

Senator Sumner had been beaten unconscious on the floor of the United States Senate by a congressman from South Carolina. "I saw him pass up Beacon Street," she wrote in her diary, "pale and feeble, but smiling and bowing." Louisa noted with delight that the Reverend Theodore Parker "cheered like a boy" for his friend. Louisa cheered, too.

Louisa was poor, and she worked hard, but she also managed to enjoy the city. Lu Willis, her cousin Hamilton's wife, took her to the opera and to a series of lectures on Italian literature. Lu also noticed Louisa's shabby old cloak and thoughtfully gave her a new scarlet one to wear in the evening instead.

Thomas Barry, the manager of the new Boston Theater, had been talking about producing a play Louisa had written from her story *The Rival Prima Donnas*. The play never was produced, but in the meantime, Mr. Barry gave Louisa a pass to use anytime

at the Boston Theater. "This was such rich-
ness I didn't care if the play was burnt on the
spot!" She danced a jig on the stage.

Louisa went to the theater, "quite stage-
struck." She was thrilled by Edwin Forrest
playing the lead in *Othello,* and Edwin T.
Booth as Brutus in *Julius Caesar.* Cousin Lu
gave her her first new silk dress, and Louisa
looked forward to wearing it to holiday parties.

Another kind of pleasure for Louisa were
the Sunday evening gatherings at the
Reverend Theodore Parker's house. Parker
knew and respected Bronson and Abby
Alcott, and he was glad to take Louisa under
his wing. A warm handshake and a kind word
from this man carried Louisa along through
the week. "He is like a great fire where all
can come and be warmed and comforted,"
she wrote in her diary. "Bless him!"

Parker and his wife welcomed some of the
most interesting people in Boston: Senator
Charles Sumner, the abolitionist William

Lloyd Garrison, the author and campaigner for women's rights Julia Ward Howe, the antislavery leader and socialist Wendell Phillips. Louisa was fascinated, although she felt a little timid in such famous company. However, back in her attic room she wrote lively descriptions of them to Anna. Mrs. Howe was "a straw colored supercilious lady with pale eyes & a green gown in which she looked like a faded lettuce."

In spite of the excitement of being on her own in Boston, Louisa was sometimes homesick. On her twenty-fourth birthday, alone in her room writing and watching the snow fall, she felt very blue. But then a letter and a pretty pin arrived from her father, who was lecturing in New York, and letters from her mother and Lizzie in New Hampshire.

Louisa was happy to return to Walpole at the end of the spring of 1857. Anna came from Syracuse to join the family, and the Alcotts were together again. Bronson's mother, Anna Alcox (Bronson had changed his last name), came from Connecticut to visit in July. "A sweet old lady," wrote Louisa in her diary. Listening to her grandmother's stories about Bronson's childhood, she understood for the first time how hard he had struggled to educate himself and make his way in the world.

By August the Alcotts were still worried about Lizzie. Unlike Abbie May, she had not really recovered from scarlet fever, and she was pale and weak. They consulted doctors, in spite of the expense, and Mrs. Alcott took Lizzie to the seashore for her health.

Bronson Alcott wanted to return to Concord, to be near his dear friend Ralph Emerson. Abby Alcott still had some money from her father's inheritance, and Emerson helped the Alcotts find and buy another house. In October the family moved from Walpole to Concord.

"Orchard House," as apple-loving Bronson

named their new home, was just up the Lexington Road from their old home, Hillside (renamed "Wayside" by Nathaniel Hawthorne). Orchard House needed a great deal of work, so the Alcotts rented half a house in the village for the winter. Louisa and Anna, ever more worried about Lizzie's health, stayed in Concord that winter to be with their sister. Bronson left on a lecture tour of New York State and Ohio.

Social life in Concord was lively that season, with dances and ice-skating parties and plays. Frank Sanborn, who ran a boys' school in Concord, organized the Concord Dramatic Union. Louisa and Anna both threw themselves into drama productions. They built scenery, sewed costumes, and took leads in most of the plays.

Through the amateur theater Louisa got to know Alf Whitman, a student of Frank Sanborn's. He was a yellow-haired boy of fifteen, the kind of younger brother Louisa had wished for when Abbie May was born instead. Anna, for her part, became very friendly with mild-mannered, handsome John Pratt, whose family was boarding Alf.

Lizzie was too weak to attend the performances, but she loved to watch her sisters get ready for the theater and hear their reports afterward. Louisa felt that she was living two lives that winter. One was full of plays and parties and fun. The other life was the sad nights she spent watching in Lizzie's bedroom, giving her mother a rest from nursing. Lizzie said she felt "strong" when Louisa was there.

Good-byes

In January 1858, Lizzie was much worse. The doctor announced what the Alcotts already knew: There was no hope. Bronson returned home from his lecture tour, and Louisa and Anna gave up plays. They wanted to spend every possible moment with their sister.

"Sad, quiet days in her room," wrote Louisa, "and strange nights keeping up the fire and watching the dear little shadow try to wile away the long sleepless hours without troubling me. She sews, reads, sings softly, and lies looking at the fire—so sweet and patient and so worn, my heart is broken to see the change."

Louisa kept her faithful watch for two months. Then Lizzie was too weak to even sew—she said the needle was "too heavy." She gave away her few possessions and kissed her mother and father and sisters good-bye. The next week, she died quietly in her sleep.

At first, Louisa was mainly relieved that Lizzie wasn't suffering any longer, and comforted to imagine her at peace in the next world. "I am glad to know she is safe from pain and age in some world where her innocent soul must be happy," she wrote in her diary.

Shortly after Lizzie's death, there was another big change in the Alcott family. Anna came home one day with her face glowing: She was engaged to John Pratt. Louisa exclaimed to herself, "I'll never forgive John for taking Anna from me!" Quickly she added, "But I shall if he makes her happy."

Now loneliness began to close in on Louisa, at home without her sisters. Lizzie was dead, Anna was at Pratt Farm with her future in-laws, and May (she had dropped "Abbie" to make her name more fashionable) was in Boston studying art. Bronson and Abby were absorbed in their new home, Orchard House.

Louisa couldn't resist poking fun at her parents. "Apple Slump," she dubbed the new Alcott residence. She had no intention of settling down in Concord, which seemed more and more of a stuffy little town to her.

But Louisa stayed in Concord to see Bronson and Abby settled in Orchard House. "We won't move again for twenty years if I can help it," she declared to her diary. "The old people need an abiding place; and now that death and love have taken two of us away, I can, I hope, soon manage to care for the remaining four." She meant herself, her parents, and May.

144

In the fall of 1858, Louisa left Concord for Mrs. Reed's boardinghouse in Boston again. She didn't know exactly how she was going to support even herself. The governess job she had hoped for did not turn up. "Every one was so busy, & cared so little whether I got work or jumped into the river that I thought seriously of doing the latter," she wrote her family later.

She had this thought one especially gloomy day, as she walked over the mill dam in Boston. She was heartsore from losing Lizzie. Her mother, once her trusted confidant, had grown so old and tired that Louisa didn't like to bother her with her problems anymore. Anna, Louisa's closest friend, had promised to share the rest of her life with John Pratt.

Staring down at the rushing water, Louisa felt overwhelmed with the goals she had set herself. A young woman of twenty-five, attempting to support her family *and* write something really great? Even one of these goals seemed far-fetched. She thought how easy it would be to just stop trying altogether. But then, Louisa wrote in her diary, "it seemed so cowardly to run away before the battle was over that I couldn't do it."

Gritting her teeth, Louisa decided to take a grueling job sewing ten hours a day at the Girls' Reform School in Lancaster, far out in the country. Just in the nick of time, she got instead the part-time job she had hoped for, as a governess in Boston. And kind Mrs. Reed offered Louisa her board in exchange for sewing. "You help so much in many ways," said her landlady, "and make it so lively."

After her moment of despair, Louisa felt stronger and more determined than ever. She was paid thirty dollars for a story called "Mark Field's Mistake," and she sent twenty dollars to her family. In a cheerful letter to Anna in November, Louisa outlined how she would spend the thirty-five dollars she had:

"I shall get a second-hand carpet for the little parlor, a bonnet for you, and some shoes and stockings for myself." Between the holes in the heels of her stockings, Louisa joked, and the holes in the toes of her shoes, she couldn't walk three times around the Common in cold weather without getting chilblains—inflamed, itchy skin.

Part of Louisa's ambitious plan for supporting her family was to launch her sister May's artistic career. That winter May, now eighteen, roomed with Louisa and studied at the Boston School of Design.

In January, Abby Alcott was ill, and Louisa took a week off to go to Concord and nurse her mother. "Wonder if I ought not to be a nurse, as I seem to have a gift for it," she wrote in her diary. Her mother, her sister Lizzie, and her cousin Lu Willis, who was asthmatic, had all told her what a wonderful nurse she was. "If I couldn't write or act I'd try it. May yet."

However, the evidence that Miss Alcott could write was steadily growing. The next fall her father, who knew James Russell Lowell, the editor of the *Atlantic Monthly*, took Lowell one of her stories. The *Atlantic* had high standards, and it would be a triumph to be published in this magazine.

"Hurrah!" Louisa exclaimed in her diary when the good news came: the *Atlantic* would publish "Love and Self-Love," and pay well for it. "Fifty dollars . . . I've not been pegging away all these years in vain, and may yet have books and publishers and a fortune of my own . . . . Twenty-seven years old, and very happy."

Meanwhile, the country was on the edge of war. Earlier that fall, the Great State Encampment brought the boom of cannon and the tramp of soldiers' boots to Concord. Louisa's blood was stirred, and she wished *she* could enlist. "I can't fight," she told herself, "but I can nurse."

The Alcotts believed that the abolitionists would have to fight to free the slaves. They admired John Brown, a fanatical preacher who planned to lead the Southern slaves in a massive uprising. That October, Brown and his abolitionist band attacked the federal arsenal at Harpers Ferry, Virginia. Brown intended to seize weapons for the slave rebellion, but instead he was captured, tried, and executed.

The Alcotts, outraged and grieved, attended a mourning service in the Concord Town Hall. Louisa wrote a poem about John Brown's death, which was published in *The Liberator.*

In the midst of such sad and threatening public events, the Alcotts celebrated their private joy. On the sunny day of May 23, 1860, the anniversary of Abby and Bronson Alcott's wedding, Anna and John were married in the parlor of Orchard House. Anna wore silver gray silk and lilies of the valley.

Uncle Sam May, who was a Unitarian minister, performed the simple ceremony. Afterward, the couple stood outside under the old chestnut tree while the guests danced around them.

"Mr. Emerson kissed her," wrote Louisa ruefully, "and I thought that honor would make even matrimony endurable."

A few weeks later, visiting Anna and John in their cottage, Louisa could see that her sister was blissfully happy. But she wasn't envious. "Very sweet and pretty," she commented to her diary, "but I'd rather be a free spinster and paddle my own canoe."

Louisa was paddling her canoe as hard as she could toward fame and fortune. Her first novel had been growing in her mind for a long time. In August she spent the whole month writing this book, *Moods*. She wrote all day and planned all night, hardly stopping to eat or sleep until she had finished the first draft.

Meanwhile, Miss Alcott's stories were fetching higher and higher prices. In September the *Atlantic Monthly* gave her seventy-five dollars for "A Modern Cinderella," a story based on the romance between Anna and John. Louisa proudly paid some of the family bills and began planning another story. Now she could "look more hopefully into the future," she wrote in her diary, "while my paper boats sailed gaily over the Atlantic."

That November Bronson Alcott turned sixty-one, and Louisa twenty-eight. They knew exactly the right presents for each other: She gave him a ream of writing paper, and he gave her a picture of Ralph Waldo Emerson.

In February 1861, Louisa went into another one of her whirlwind writing spurts. For three weeks she sat at the desk in her upstairs bedroom at Orchard House, rewriting the manuscript of *Moods*. Her mother tiptoed into the room with cups of tea, and her father brought her apples and cider.

Losing herself in her writing was thrilling, like riding a flying horse. But by the time she finally put down her pen, Louisa was dizzy from lack of food, her legs shook, and she couldn't sleep. When she had recovered a bit, she read her novel to her father and mother and Anna. "It was worth something," she told her diary, "to have my three dearest sit up till midnight listening with wide-open eyes to Lu's first novel."

In the outside world, it seemed that the country would be torn apart. Abraham Lincoln had been elected president by less than half the voters, and the Southern states had formed their own nation, the Confederacy. In April, war broke out.

Louisa cheered the young men of Concord as they left to join the Union army. With the other women of Concord, she sewed uniforms and knitted socks for the soldiers, but she was not satisfied. She wished she were a man, so that she, too, could risk her life fighting slavery.

Louisa tried writing for the cause, but it only frustrated her. The poem she had written on the death of John Brown couldn't express what she felt. Remembering Anthony Burns's scarred face, she wrote a story about a runaway slave. But the *Atlantic Monthly* refused to publish an abolitionist story. "The dear South must not be offended," Louisa noted sarcastically in her diary.

In 1862, Elizabeth Peabody, still a power in Boston education, persuaded Louisa to open a kindergarten in the city. The editor James T. Fields also thought this was a good idea, and he lent her forty dollars to furnish the school. Louisa taught the kindergarten from January through April, but it didn't pay even well enough for her to support herself.

Louisa laughed as she remembered Mr. Fields's patronizing words, almost ten years ago, after reading her story about her miserable experience in Dedham: "Stick to your teaching, Miss Alcott. You can't write." In fact, by this time she could make much better money writing. She quit teaching, and never returned to it.

That fall Louisa proudly wrote in her diary, "Mr. L. says my tales are so 'dramatic, vivid, and full of plot,' they are just what he wants." "Mr. L." was Frank Leslie, editor of the immensely popular *Frank Leslie's Illustrated Newspaper*. Louisa later made fun of these sensational stories in a letter to Alf Whitman, warning him that an illustration of one of her stories might show "Indians, pirates, wolves, bears & distressed damsels in a grand tableau over a title like this: "The Maniac Bride" or "The Bath of Blood." She didn't care, because Leslie paid well. And he would publish her "blood and thunder" stories as fast as she could write them.

This personal success was sweet. But the war was not going well for the Union. The second Battle of Bull Run, in August, had been a Confederate victory. The Battle of Antietam in September was a draw, but a terrible slaughter, with thousands of Union soldiers killed. More than ever, Louisa longed to do her part in the fight to free the slaves—more of a part than rolling bandages and knitting socks.

"I Can't Fight, But I Can Nurse"

In the second year of the Civil War, the military hospitals were overflowing with wounded soldiers. Louisa heard that strong, mature women were being recruited to nurse them. "Thirty years old," she wrote in her diary in November 1862. "Decided to go to Washington as nurse if I could find a place. Help needed, and I love nursing, and must let out my pent-up energy in some new way."

While she waited for the answer to

her application, Louisa studied Florence Nightingale's *Notes on Nursing*. She was eager to put into practice Nightingale's principles about fresh air and clean rooms.

In December, Louisa received her orders. She was to report to the Union Hospital in Washington, D.C., where she would work for three months for room and board and twelve dollars a month. She packed drab, sturdy clothes to work in, and books and games to amuse the sick soldiers.

Saying good-bye to her family in Concord, Louisa looked at her mother's tear-streaked face. It struck her with full force: Nursing was dangerous work. She might easily die from working in a military hospital, and she would be just as dead as if she had been shot on the battlefield. She might never see that dear face again.

Louisa hugged her mother tightly. "Shall I stay?"

"No, go," Mrs. Alcott answered through

her sobs, "and the Lord be with you!"

Louisa took the train from Concord into Boston, another train from Boston to New London, Connecticut, a ferry through Long Island Sound to Jersey City, and then another train south through Philadelphia and Baltimore. Nearing Washington, D.C., she stared out the window at a countryside covered with army tents.

At last, on the third day of her journey, she arrived after dark at the Union Hospital, a former hotel in Georgetown. The drafty little room she was to share with two other nurses contained "narrow iron beds, spread with thin mattresses like plasters, and furnished with pillows in the last stages of consumption," she wrote home. Over the washstand hung a mirror the size of "a muffin, and about as reflective."

The next day, Louisa set to work before daylight. Union Hospital was a cold, damp, dirty, stinking place. No one seemed to be in charge. Without any kind of introduction, Louisa was given a ward of forty beds, a section of the former hotel's ballroom.

At first, Louisa felt bashful and awkward. Washing strange men was a far cry from tending a sick member of her own family. But her heart went out to the suffering soldiers, and they responded gratefully.

On her first shift, Louisa saw a man die. She spent most of that day with two patients: a man shot through the lungs, staring silently at her with large dark eyes, and a boy gasping with pneumonia. "You are real motherly, ma'am," said the boy as she wrapped a shawl around his shoulders.

Only a few days after Louisa's arrival, a long line of ambulances from the disastrous Battle of Fredericksburg pulled up in front of the hospital. Louisa and the other nurses worked like cart horses. All day long she trotted from one end of the ward to another. Besides the expected nursing work—washing the patients, feeding them, changing the dressing on their wounds, and assisting the doctors—she had all kinds of housekeeping duties. She even had to show the attendants how to make beds and sweep floors.

Louisa had always liked to stay up late at night, and she soon took over the night shift in her ward. This arrangement gave her time for a run in the morning, in the fresh air. She also exercised during pauses in her work, walking up and down the halls of the hotel, while the men were all asleep. The solitude gave her a chance to "write" in her head, and during one of these nights she composed a poem about her old friend Henry Thoreau, who had died in Concord last spring.

The part of nursing Louisa loved most was getting to know each patient individually and doing whatever she could to cheer him. She wrote letters for soldiers who couldn't hold a pen; she read to them. She made them laugh by quoting funny passages from Charles

Dickens's novels. One man, discharged from the hospital, told her he was sorry to leave—he'd had no idea a hospital was such a jolly place. He was hoping to get wounded again, he joked, and come back and be taken care of by Nurse Alcott.

Louisa spent that Christmas Eve caring for a young sergeant who had lost an arm and a leg at Fredericksburg. She held the lamp for the doctor as he changed the dressing on the stump of Sergeant Bane's arm. All three of them chatted and laughed to take the man's mind off his pain.

Besides their wounds, the soldiers suffered from a host of diseases: pneumonia, diptheria, typhoid fever. No wonder, thought Louisa, as she ran around opening windows in an attempt to get some fresh air for herself and the men. "A more perfect pestilence-box than this house I never saw—cold, damp, dirty, full of vile odors from wounds, kitchens, washrooms, and stables."

* * *

After weeks of exhausting work in the crowded, unsanitary wards, Louisa began to feel tired and dizzy. She often had to pause in the middle of her work, racked with coughs. Finally the doctor ordered her to stay in her room.

Still, when church bells rang in the New Year of 1863, Louisa jumped out of bed and ran to the window. Down in the streets, black people were celebrating with firecrackers and horns, shouting and singing. Louisa cheered feebly, too, and waved her handkerchief out the window. This January first would begin a truly new year. President Lincoln was going to make the Emancipation Proclamation, setting free all the slaves in Confederate territory.

In order to work for this cause she believed in so deeply, Louisa had put aside her ambition for the time being. Still, she had her own private good news to celebrate. She had won first prize—one hundred dollars!—in *Frank Leslie's Illustrated Newspaper*'s story contest with "Pauline's Passion and Punishment."

Louisa hoped to get over her illness quickly and go back to work in the hospital. Instead, she got worse. She was too sick to eat, and her feverish mind wandered. Everyone advised her to leave, but Louisa was determined to stick out the three months she had signed up for. Against her wishes, another nurse finally sent a telegram to the Alcotts in Concord.

One day Louisa was startled by what could have been another fever vision: her silver-haired father's kindly face. Bronson Alcott had come to take his daughter home, before she died in this wretched little room. After the head nurse actually did die of typhoid fever, Louisa allowed herself to be taken away on the long journey north.

Faces appeared to Louisa as if out of

nowhere: strangers staring at her at the Boston station, then her sister May's shocked face as Louisa stumbled off the train at Concord. At Orchard House, she met her mother's worn, bewildered face. Louisa was too far gone to understand that it was her own thin, white, blank face—ordinarily so expressive—that horrified them.

For three weeks Louisa's mother and father and May took turns nursing her, as tenderly as Louisa had nursed the soldiers in the Union Hospital. Finally her fever ebbed, but it left her too weak to even walk. She was shocked to see herself in the mirror, "a queer, thin, big-eyed face" she hardly recognized.

And Louisa's "one beauty," as she called it, her yard and a half of thick, glossy, chestnut-colored hair, had been cut off. "Never mind," she wrote in her diary. "It might have been my head."

Now she had to recover not only from her illness but also from the medicine she had taken. That was calomel, which contained the poison mercury. At the time, doctors did not realize that mercury is not flushed out of the body, but remains to cause problems later. Even after Louisa was strong enough to get out of bed, she ached all over and had trouble sleeping.

In March, as Louisa was slowly returning to health, all the Alcotts received a great boost to their spirits. Bronson Alcott burst in the door of Orchard House one night, powdered with snow from the storm outside, with the good news. Anna and John's first child had been born—a boy, Frederick Alcott Pratt.

"We opened our mouths and screamed for about two minutes," Louisa wrote Anna. "Then Mother began to cry, I began to laugh, and May to pour out questions; while Papa beamed upon us all."

In April, Louisa took stock. She was not really well, but there was work to be done.

166

For three weeks of service at Union Hospital and two months of near-fatal illness, the government had paid her only ten dollars. Louisa was still the breadwinner of the family, and the debts were piling up again.

At her friend Frank Sanborn's suggestion, Louisa found a way to turn her nursing experience into good money, after all. She rewrote the letters she had sent home from the hospital, and they were published in Sanborn's *Boston Commonwealth* as "Hospital Sketches." To her surprise, they were a hit, and she received many letters about them. She was especially glad to hear from brave Sergeant Bane, one of the men she had nursed at Union Hospital, now home in Michigan.

With her forty dollars for "Hospital Sketches" and the one-hundred-dollar prize for "Pauline's Passion and Punishment," Louisa felt she had made a respectable start on her earnings for the year, in spite of almost dying. More important, she was getting a sense of the kind of writing she did best: not the made-up melodramas, the "blood-and-thunder" stories, but the real dramas she knew from her own life.

Hospital Sketches was published as a book, and Louisa's reputation grew steadily. She could sell all the stories she wrote now, for a good price. Her poem "Thoreau's Flute," commemorating Henry Thoreau, was published by the *Atlantic Monthly*, and she had new hopes for her novel, *Moods*. Proudly Louisa paid for May's train fare to her drawing lessons in Boston and outfitted her stylish younger sister in new hat, boots, gloves, and ribbons. "Fifteen years of hard grubbing may be coming to something after all; and I may yet 'pay all the debts, fix the house, send May to Italy, and keep the old folks cozy,' as I've said I would so long, yet so hopelessly," Louisa wrote in her diary.

Moods was published at the end of 1864 and sold fairly well. The Alcotts were happy and busy: Bronson was regularly invited to speak now; Anna was absorbed in her boy, Freddie, and expecting another baby. Abby was delighted to be a grandmother, and May to pursue her artistic career. Louisa wrote, and acted in theatricals for charity, and was welcomed at parties as one of Boston's literary set.

But Louisa's stint at the military hospital, although it almost killed her, had whetted her appetite for new experiences. For many years she had longed to see Europe. In July 1865, the month after the birth of her second nephew, John Pratt, Jr., she was invited to go to Europe, expenses paid. She would be the companion and nurse of a wealthy young invalid, Anna Weld.

During the year she spent in Europe, Louisa realized some of her dreams. She walked the streets of Charles Dickens's London and even heard Dickens himself read. In Frankfurt, she visited the house of the German author Goethe. She reveled in the dramatic scenery of the Rhine River and the Alps. But she was bored by the long stays with Miss Weld at health spas, and irritated at being tied down to an invalid for months on end.

An unexpected bonus of the trip was a new friend, Ladislas Wisniewski, whom Louisa met at Vevey, a resort on Lake Lucerne in Switzerland. She liked the young Polish man as much as she had liked Alf Whitman in the old Concord days. He was a lively, charming lad of twenty, a talented pianist, with dark eyes and dark curly hair. She nicknamed him Laurie, and they spent many hours taking long walks and sailing on the lake.

After a tedious winter on the French Riviera with Anna Weld, Louisa quit her nurse/companion job and set off to enjoy herself, in spite of the expense. She spent two weeks in Paris, sightseeing with Ladislas. Then Louisa went on to London, and spent a month and a half there. "Very free and jolly, roaming about London all day, dining late and resting, chatting, music, or fun in the evening."

In July 1866, Louisa returned to Orchard House in Concord for a joyous reunion with her father, her mother, May, and Anna and John and their two little boys. But before long the author was back at her desk. "Soon fell to work on some stories," she noted in her diary, "for things were, as I expected, behindhand when the money-maker was away."

Little Women

Returning from Europe, Louisa had been shocked to see that Abby Alcott, the "strong, energetic Marmee," had turned into a bent, wrinkled old woman. "Life has been so hard for her, and she so brave, so glad to spend herself for others," wrote Louisa in her diary. "Now we must live for her."

But living for her family didn't necessarily mean that Louisa had to live *with* them in Concord. By the fall of 1867, she was restless again to be in a city. Besides, her health wasn't always good, and she craved privacy. In

Concord, her work was interrupted by strangers appearing at Orchard House and demanding to see the "authoress."

So Louisa moved once more into Boston, to a room of her own on Hayward Place, off Washington Street, conveniently near her publishers. Louisa had come a long way from the days of her little attic room at the top of Mrs. Reed's boardinghouse. These days, she didn't have to scrimp to buy shoes and stockings. Horace Fuller had asked her to edit his magazine for children, *Merry's Museum*, for five hundred dollars a year.

Editor Thomas Niles at Roberts Brothers Publishers had also suggested a new project: He wanted Miss Alcott to write a book for girls. "Said I'd try," noted Louisa in her diary.

Louisa wasn't excited about the idea of writing a book for girls. Outside of her sisters, her own best friends had always been boys. Anyway, she had so many other writing projects.

There were the guaranteed moneymakers, her "blood-and-thunder" stories for publications like *Frank Leslie's Illustrated Newspaper*. And there were serious topics dear to her heart. In "Happy Women," an article she wrote in February for *The New York Ledger*, she praised unmarried women who find a satisfying life through their work. She knew many "busy, useful, independent spinsters," and she was one herself. "Liberty is a better husband than love to many of us," she wrote.

On the other hand, when she played with her nephews, Freddy, now almost five, and Johnny, two and a half, Louisa was keenly aware of what she had given up. "She is a happy woman!" she sighed to her diary after a visit to Anna. "I sell *my* children, and though they feed me, they don't love me as hers do."

A "child" Louisa had had great hopes for was *Moods*, a serious novel about love and marriage. It had been published the year before her trip to Europe. She had worked hard on it, writing and rewriting and revising much more than usual. But she wasn't really happy with this story. It wasn't written from her own experience, except her experience of observing other people's marriages. She had noticed, she said, that "very few were happy ones."

By the end of February 1868, besides editing the magazine *Merry's Museum*, Louisa had written eight long stories and ten short ones. On top of that, she had acted twelve times in charity performances. "Not a bad two months work," she noted in her diary. Living in Boston by herself, writing without distractions, suited her very well. Reluctantly she went back to Concord to take care of her mother, who was ill.

In May, Louisa asked Roberts Brothers if they would be interested in a book of fairy tales. No, answered editor Thomas Niles—

but he still thought she should write a book for girls, about real girls.

Louisa had made a start on that book last September, but she wasn't enthusiastic about it. But her mother and sisters thought it was a good idea, and her publisher was willing to pay for it. So Louisa sat down at her writing desk by the window in her upstairs bedroom at Orchard House. She began to "plod away," as she put it, at this book for girls.

She planned to tell the story of four sisters with poor but loving parents. They would live in a house like Orchard House, in a town like Concord. The family would be named—"March," she decided, which hinted at her mother's family name, May.

Once Louisa got going, the story poured out as fast as she could scribble. The Marches, like the Alcotts, would compare their lives to *Pilgrim's Progress*. They would struggle through the Slough of Despond, and be tempted by the empty pleasures of Vanity

176

Fair, and face down the Giant Despair. They would strive (not always successfully) to become better people.

The oldest girl, Meg, was like Louisa's sister Anna—ladylike and domestic, but with a great sense of fun. The youngest sister was artistic and blue eyed, with blond curls, like May. Also like May, she was a bit spoiled, and apt to make funny mistakes when she gave herself airs. Louisa named this character by rearranging the letters in "May" to "Amy." The second youngest sister was shy and sweet, wanting only to live for her family. Louisa kept her real name, Elizabeth, but nicknamed her "Beth" instead of Lizzie.

And for the second oldest sister, Jo, Louisa simply looked in the mirror. Jo was tall and thin, with sharp gray eyes and a mane of thick, shiny brown hair. Full of energy and ambition, she was dismayed by the ups and downs of her feelings and by her fierce bursts of temper. Jo, like Louisa, often wished she had been born a boy.

Jo's best friend, beside her sisters, was the boy next door. Laurie was a mix of Alf Whitman, Louisa's good friend from the old days in Concord, and Ladislas Wisniewski, the charming Polish youth with dark eyes and dark curly hair. Laurie's grandfather, a gruff but kind gentleman, was modeled on Louisa's own grandfather, Joseph May.

The strong, devoted Mrs. March in Louisa's story was a "stout, motherly lady, with a 'can-I-help-you' look about her"— much like Abby Alcott, only wiser and more serene. Like Mrs. Alcott, Mrs. March earned part of the family income as a relief worker. She was deeply concerned about poor people, and the March family, like the Alcotts, would be exposed to scarlet fever through her care for a poverty-stricken neighbor.

The father of the March family was loving but, like Bronson Alcott, not there much of the time. Louisa sent Mr. March off to the Civil War and had him fall ill in an army hospital, as she had done. Also like Bronson, Mr. March was not much good at making a living. But Louisa tactfully decided that Mr. March had "lost his property in trying to help an unfortunate friend."

Bending over her desk with its view of the Lexington Road, Louisa wrote and wrote. She wrote through the month of May, then June. When she sent the first twelve chapters to Thomas Niles, he thought they were "dull."

"So do I," admitted Louisa to her diary. Still, now that she had gotten into the lives of the Marches, she was determined to finish. "Lively simple books are very much needed for girls, and perhaps I can supply the need."

Louisa was discovering that her own life had been full of drama and excitement, although not exactly "blood and thunder." The Alcott girls had always struggled to earn money for the family, and so would Meg and Jo. Jo would lose her hair, her "one beauty," as Louisa had lost hers during her battle with typhoid fever. All the fun of growing up as Alcotts—the plays in the barn and parlor, the wild games, the celebrations of birthdays and Christmas—would be the Marches' fun, too.

By the middle of July, Louisa was exhausted, and her head ached badly. But she had finished the first part of her family saga, 402 pages, ending with Meg's engagement to John Brooke, a man very much like John Pratt. As Thomas Niles suggested, she called the book *Little Women*.

Niles was still a bit doubtful, but he accepted the book for publication. When he let some girls read the manuscript, *they* had no doubts at all. "Splendid!" was their reaction.

What these first readers loved so much were Jo and Meg and Beth and Amy—*real* girls with all their faults and all their good qualities. And the Marches were a real family:

working together, playing together, quarreling, making up. They helped each other through the hard times and celebrated the good ones, as the Alcotts always had.

Louisa herself, reading the page proofs, liked *Little Women* better than she had expected. "We really lived most of it," she commented, "and if it succeeds that will be the reason of it."

The book was published in October. By the end of the month the first printing had sold out, and a London publisher had arranged to publish *Little Women* in England. Thomas Niles urged Louisa to write a second volume right away, so that he could publish it in the spring.

On November 1, Louisa got to work on *Little Women,* Part II, planning to write a chapter a day. She refused to marry Jo to Laurie, as many of her readers wanted her to. In fact, she wasn't eager to marry off any of her "little women." Neither were Mr. and

Mrs. March. "Better be happy old maids than unhappy wives," Marmee tells Meg and Jo early in *Little Women*.

Louisa had Amy travel to Europe, to see the great sights of the Old World and to study art. Jo she sent off to New York, as Louisa had gone off to Boston by herself, to earn her own living and write. Like Anna, Meg began married life, and had two children. And Beth died, as the real-life Lizzie had died, of complications from scarlet fever.

For her readers who wanted romance, Louisa compromised by matching Amy with Laurie, and finally Jo with Professor Fritz Bhaer. In personality the German professor was a bit like her hero Mr. Emerson, and a bit like Bronson Alcott.

Finished with Part II of *Little Women*, Louisa tried to rest. She was boneweary, racked with coughs and aches. "Paid up all the debts, thank the Lord!" she wrote in her diary in March 1869. The second volume of

Little Women was published in April, with four thousand copies pre-sold. (The version of *Little Women* we know today includes Part I and Part II.)

Miss Alcott's readers and publishers wanted another book, but Louisa was afraid of going into one of her weeks-long writing spurts and getting really ill. On the other hand, she was afraid to stop working. "The family seem so panic-stricken and helpless when I break down, that I try to keep the mill going."

Louisa began another book for girls, this time about Polly, a girl from the country who comes to the city to live with a wealthy friend. It was a good chance to make fun of everything Louisa thought was silly about fashionable life: fancy hairdos, uncomfortable and impractical clothes, young girls imitating society belles. The city friend has a brother, a mischievous fourteen-year-old of the kind Louisa liked so well. The story is full of humorous pranks and mishaps.

At the beginning of 1870, Louisa was tormented by ill health. She lost her voice, and her doctor prescribed a harsh treatment that seared her throat. She suffered from headaches, and because of rheumatism she had to write with one foot up and her left hand in a sling. But by February she had finished *An Old-Fashioned Girl*, and it was published in March. Delighted readers asked her, "Didn't you enjoy doing it?"

Exhausted and still not well, Louisa was plagued with the newspaper reporters who came to Concord to interview the famous Miss Alcott. She now understood why the author Nathaniel Hawthorne used to hide from visitors in the woods behind his house, because she started doing the same thing. What she really needed was to get away for a change and a rest. She decided to treat herself to a tour of Europe, and take May with her.

In April, Louisa and May rode the train from Boston to New York, escorted by their

brother-in-law, John Pratt. A boy came through the cars selling books, including *An Old-Fashioned Girl*. "I don't care for it," said Louisa, to amuse John and May.

"Bully book, ma'am!" the boy assured her. "Sell a lot; better have it."

From New York, Louisa and May sailed to France on the steamship *Lafayette*. The weather was cold and rainy, the seas were rough, and Louisa was so seasick that she joked the ship should have been named the *Nausea*. Several girls on board were reading *An Old-Fashioned Girl*. When they found out the author was on board, they came in an awestruck group to visit her in her cabin.

Little Men

That November Louisa celebrated her thirty-eighth birthday in Rome, in an apartment overlooking the fountain of the Triton. Although she was still bothered by rheumatic pain, it was a happy birthday in many ways. She was exploring Europe again, this time free to go exactly where she wished. She had the pleasure, at last, of seeing her talented youngest sister study the Old Masters of European art.

Louisa didn't need to worry about money, for the sales of *Little Women* continued to mount. And *An Old-Fashioned Girl* had been selling briskly ever since its publication in June.

But while Louisa and May were enjoying themselves in Rome, tragic news came across the Atlantic. John Pratt, who had seen them off from the docks in New York, had suddenly fallen ill and died on November 27. Anna was a widow with two young boys.

Grieving, Louisa sent Anna a tender letter about how much John had meant to her. "He did more to make us trust & respect men than any one I know," she wrote. "No born brother was ever dearer, & each year I loved & respected & admired him more & more."

One part of Louisa longed to rush home and comfort her family. But it was winter, and the long journey would strain her health. Also, she knew she could work better if she stayed in Rome. She had already begun writing a new book, *Little Men*, a sequel to *Little Women*.

Now Louisa got to work with fresh energy, thinking of the money needed to support her nephews and Anna and to pay for the boys' education. "Long ago," she explained to a friend, "I promised to try and fill John's place if they were left fatherless." "To Freddy and Johnny," she wrote on the dedication page of her new book, "the Little Men to whom she owes some of the best and happiest hours of her life, this book is gratefully dedicated by their loving 'Aunt Weedy.'"

Little Men is the story of the boys at Plumfield, a boarding school and farm run by Jo of *Little Women* and her husband, Fritz Bhaer. Although Louisa had decided long ago that she didn't want to be a teacher, she must have loved imagining a school for boys. If she were young and healthy, like Jo, it would be great fun to have a whole big houseful of children.

Like the Alcotts, Jo and her husband welcome children who might not fit in anywhere else. One boy has a crooked spine, and another has a serious learning disability. They also take in Nat, abandoned by an abusive uncle, and Dan, a tough street boy. The Bhaers expect the boys to obey the few rules of the school, but they also allow Saturday night pillow fights. And they encourage outdoor exercise and work as well as studying.

Plumfield is run along Bronson Alcott's principles of education. "We don't believe in making children miserable by too many rules, and too much study," Jo explains to Nat. She and her husband believe in teaching by gentle encouragement. In one scene in *Little Men*, Professor Bhaer makes Nat, who has told a lie, strike him with a ruler. Just like the boys at Bronson's Temple School, Nat finds this punishment much harder to take than being hit himself.

Because the Bhaers are truly interested in each boy, the boys try their best to please them. The Bhaers also believe that teaching the boys to know themselves and to work toward self-improvement is as important as arithmetic or Latin. These ideas had seemed outlandish when Bronson Alcott taught the children at the Temple School, and they were still highly unusual in 1870.

One of the few girls at Plumfield is Nan, as wild and rebellious—and as bright and tenderhearted—as Louisa used to be. Like young Louy, Nan likes to race the boys and beat them. She thinks up the most interesting games—instead of playing quietly with her doll, she turns it into an Indian chief and has it massacre the other dolls.

With the same kind of sympathy that Louisa's mother had for her, Jo sees not only Nan's wildness but her courage and her talent. Nan has a clear gift for treating sick people. Although women doctors were almost unheard of then, Jo encourages Nan to prepare for studying medicine.

Dan, the wildest of the boys, strikes up a

friendship with a man like Henry Thoreau, who can make birds come to him, and knows everything about fish and flies and Indians and rocks. With Jo's support, Dan discovers his own calling as a naturalist.

In Rome, so far away from her family, grieving for her brother-in-law, Louisa must have found comfort in remembering the games and romps of her own childhood. In one chapter, Jo's nephew invents a spirit, the "Naughty Kitty-mouse," which demands burned sacrifices of their toys. Louisa remembered the Alcott theatricals, too, and gave several pages of *Little Men* to an elaborate production of "Cinderella," complete with an enormous real pumpkin.

As she neared the end of *Little Men*, Louisa honored John Pratt in describing the death of his fictional double, John Brooke. Writing in her rooms on the Piazza Barbarini, she imagined all the family and friends at his simple funeral in Concord, and what they would say in praise of this "busy, quiet, humble" man. She had Jo's Plumfield boys sing the hymn at the end of the service in a heartfelt chorus.

Returning from Europe in June of 1871, Louisa was met at the dock in Boston by her father and her editor, Thomas Niles. *Little Men* was already in print, as a red sign in the carriage announced. In fact, fifty thousand copies of Miss Alcott's new book had been pre-sold.

Although her main concern was her family, Louisa couldn't stand to stay in Concord for long. She moved back into Boston, where she could concentrate on her writing. In December 1871 she wrote proudly in her diary: "My long-cherished dream has come true, for [Mother] sits in a pleasant room, with no work, no care, no poverty to worry, but peace and comfort all about her." Louisa paid off all the family debts and then bought a furnace to make Orchard House cozy.

Another great satisfaction for Louisa was the letters she got from her young fans. "Over a hundred letters from boys and girls," she wrote in 1872, "& many from teachers & parents assure me that my little books are read & valued in a way I never dreamed of seeing them. This success is more agreeable to me than money or reputation."

However, that didn't mean Louisa was willing to give up her privacy. "People must learn that authors have some rights," she exclaimed to her diary in August 1872. Even more than before, Louisa was annoyed by sight-seekers in Concord. Reporters felt free to sit on the garden wall and take notes on the famous author.

Louisa resented being interrupted by sight-seekers while she was trying to write. Now she was rewriting a novel, *Work*, that she had begun back in 1861. This book was based on her own struggles as a young woman to earn an independent living.

Again, Louisa felt cautious about letting herself go on another of her intense writing spurts, in which she would hardly eat or sleep. If her health broke down, there was no one else to support the family. On the other hand, the *Christian Union* had offered her three thousand dollars for the story, and she couldn't refuse. "Can't work slowly," she noted in her diary. "The thing possesses me, and I must obey till it's done."

The three thousand was dearly earned. By gripping a pen for fourteen hours at a stretch, Louisa permanently injured her right thumb. She learned to write holding the pen with two fingers.

Sometimes as Louisa wrote she was also nursing her mother, who was often ill. She finished *Work* early in 1873, in spite of spending several weeks nursing her sister Anna back from a bout with pneumonia. Later in the year, Abby Alcott was ill and needed Louisa's care again.

In the fall Louisa sent May back to London to continue her art studies, and Bronson Alcott was off to the West on another lecture tour. These days, he could expect to be welcomed as the "grandfather of *Little Women*," as he proudly told Louisa. As for the rest of the family, Louisa felt she couldn't leave them in Concord for the winter, so she brought her mother and Anna and her boys to Boston.

In March 1874, Louisa was happy to welcome May back from London and see the progress she had made as an artist. It was also a relief to let May take over keeping house in Concord and caring for their mother for a few months. Louisa moved into Boston, to rest and write.

After the success of *Little Women*, Louisa had sent James T. Fields the forty dollars that he lent her nine years ago to start a kindergarten. She enclosed a saucy note, referring to the "miracle" that allowed her to repay the debt. Fields laughed and good-naturedly admitted he had misjudged Miss Alcott's writing ability.

In June 1874, Louisa took a particular pleasure in publishing a story titled "How I Went Out to Service." It was the tale of her miserable experience as a domestic servant in Dedham, the same story that had prompted Fields to tell her to stick to her teaching. As a struggling young writer, Louisa would have been happy to receive five dollars for "How I Went Out to Service." Now the *Independent* paid her two hundred dollars for it. This was a double triumph for Louisa: over the "gentleman" who had harassed and exploited her, and over the editor who didn't know a born writer when he saw one.

In the fall of 1874, Louisa rented rooms at the Hotel Bellevue in Boston for herself and May. May, now an accomplished artist, could give drawing lessons in one room, while Louisa wrote in the other. Louisa had begun another book, and Mary Mapes Dodge, author of *Hans Brinker, or the Silver Skates*, was waiting to serialize it in her new magazine, *St. Nicholas*. This book, *Eight Cousins*, was about a girl growing up with her boy cousins in a big, jolly family compound nicknamed the "Aunt-Hill."

Rose of *Eight Cousins* is an orphan, the ward of her Uncle Alec. Uncle Alec, like Louisa, thinks that tight corsets are ridiculous and harmful. He also believes, as the Alcotts always had, in wholesome food and plenty of fresh air, sunshine, and exercise for both boys and girls.

"Tried to work on my book, but was in such pain could not do much," Louisa wrote in her diary in October. She was unable to sleep without heavy doses of pain medication. In a letter to young fans, she described herself as "a tired out old lady of 42 with nothing left of her youth but a yard or more of chestnut hair that *won't* turn gray though it is time it did."

However, Louisa could still chuckle over the fact that *three* publishers were fighting each other for this book she hadn't even written yet. "No more peddling poor little manuscripts now, and feeling rich with $10," she crowed. The next year, *Eight Cousins* was finished and in print in spite of the author's bad health.

Success

In the decades after the Civil War, there was a surge of renewed interest in women's rights. Louisa, of course, had never *lost* interest. When Lucy Stone of the *Women's Journal* wrote in October 1873, asking whether Miss Alcott was for women's suffrage, the right to vote, Louisa assured her that she was. And so were her mother and father, as they always had been, and the rest of her family. Louisa couldn't resist mentioning the encouraging words of her nephews, now nine and seven: "Go ahead, Aunt Weedy, we will let you vote as much as you like."

The next year, Louisa wrote encouraging a friend, Maria Porter, who had just been elected to her town's school committee. Louisa hoped Mrs. Porter's first action would be to reduce the salary of the high school headmaster and to raise the salary of his female assistant, who worked harder. "I believe in the same pay for the same good work," she wrote.

In February 1875, Louisa visited Vassar College, a school founded on the radical idea that young women had a right to higher education. Now Vassar was celebrating its tenth anniversary, and Miss Alcott was invited as an honored guest. Louisa refused to give a speech, but she was glad to visit the observatory and talk with Maria Mitchell, the professor of astronomy. And she couldn't refuse to autograph stacks of albums for her eager young fans.

In April, when Concord celebrated the

one-hundreth anniversary of the famous Battle of Concord, Louisa joined the women's protest. Although the women of the town paid taxes to support the centennial celebration, they were not welcomed at the festivities. Worse, they were still not allowed to vote in Concord. Louisa wrote an indignant report of the event for the *Women's Journal*.

That fall, Louisa attended the Women's Congress in Syracuse, New York. She tried to stay out of sight, but she was discovered and mobbed by young women clamoring for her autograph and by people begging her to visit them.

One woman in the crowd gushed, "If you ever come to Oshkosh, your feet will not be allowed to touch the ground: you will be borne in the arms of the people! Will you come?"

"Never," said Louisa, trying not to laugh.

From Syracuse, Louisa went on to New York City for a two-month stay at a spa hotel, where she could take Turkish baths. Feeling healthy and energetic for a change, Louisa thoroughly enjoyed herself. The leaders of literary and social reform circles welcomed the famous Miss Alcott to New York, and she was invited to many meetings and lectures and parties. She drove in Central Park, and went to the theater several times. Still, she managed to write a few short stories in between.

On November 26, Louisa wrote her father a long, newsy letter, about her doings in New York, for their joint birthday. "Dear Seventy-six," she addressed him, and she signed the letter, "Ever your loving Forty-three."

But the outings Louisa enjoyed most in New York were her visits to charities, such as a home for orphan newsboys. She wrote a vivid description of the Newsboys' Lodging Home to her nephews, Fred and Johnny. She was touched and impressed by these "little men," some of them as young as nine, already earning their own living.

The next summer, back in her upstairs bedroom in the Orchard House again, Louisa wrote *Rose in Bloom*, the sequel to *Eight Cousins*, in three weeks. Rose, the heroine, chooses to spend her wealth on helping other people rather than amusing herself in society. When *Rose in Bloom* was published that November, Louisa only noted in her diary, "Sells well." She was getting used to success.

With all the money she was earning now, Louisa was able to send May off for another year of studying art in London and Paris. The next spring, she helped buy a house in Concord for Anna and her boys. Louisa was glad for Anna, just as she was glad for May. But a pang of envy burst out in her diary entry of April 1877: "So she has *her* wish, and is happy. When shall I have mine? Ought to be contented with knowing I help both sisters by my brains. But I'm selfish, and want to go away and rest in Europe. Never shall."

By September, Abby Alcott was very ill and

expected to die soon. Louisa stayed in Concord and watched by the sickbed, but she also managed to write more stories. She worked hard to finish a new book, *Under the Lilacs.* "Brain very lively and pen flew," she noted in her diary.

"Stay by, Louy," begged her mother, "and help me if I suffer too much." Louy stayed, although she became exhausted and had to collapse into bed herself for a time. The family wanted to let May know her mother was dying, so that she could come home to say good-bye, but Abby would not allow it.

On the rainy Sunday of November 25, shortly before Louisa's and Bronson's birthday, Abby Alcott died in her daughter's arms. Louisa was glad her mother was out of pain at last, but she was very low in spirits that winter. "A great warmth seems gone out of life," she wrote, "and there is no motive to go on now."

The sadness of Abby Alcott's death was followed, early in 1878, by good news from

May. She was engaged to a young Swiss man, Ernest Nieriker, whom she had gotten to know in London. They were married in March, and went to live in France.

So May would not be returning to Orchard House anytime soon. Louisa and Anna and Bronson missed her badly, and May missed her family in America. But she loved French life, and she was "unspeakably happy," as she put it, with her husband.

Louisa couldn't help feeling envious. "How different our lives are just now!—I so lonely, sad, and sick; she so happy, well, and blest." Much of the time now, Louisa was too ill to enjoy the parties and dramatic readings she used to revel in.

With all the demands on her time, Louisa was generous with advice for young writers. She told one boy, who had sent her a romantic story, that his writing was better than most. But she encouraged him to write about what he understood and to try to use short, strong words rather than fancy ones. "Read Ralph Waldo Emerson," she added, "and see what good prose is."

One of Louisa's worries was her father, who had been devastated by the death of his wife of forty-seven years. She encouraged Bronson to make plans for one of his fondest dreams, the Concord School of Philosophy. In July 1879, the silver-haired "sage of Concord" opened his school to thirty students. Louisa was happy for her father, with his disciples and "plenty of talk to swim in." But she got very tired of the "budding philosophers" swarming around Concord.

In Louisa's opinion, all that talk was a waste of time, when there was so much real work to be done—feeding the poor, for instance. Or getting women the right to vote. Louisa, chairwoman of the Concord Women's Suffrage Society, was the first to register at the Concord Town Hall that summer.

Louisa longed to visit her younger sister in

France, especially after May became pregnant. Louisa and Anna happily sewed baby clothes to send, joking that May would probably dress the baby in artist's canvas if it were left up to her. Louisa made plans to visit May, but had to cancel them, afraid that travel would strain her health. In November, May had a baby girl and named her Louisa May Nieriker.

At first, the Alcotts rejoiced. But then came the news that May was ill from complications of childbirth. She died on December 29. Ernest Niericker sent a telegram to Ralph Emerson, and he broke the sad news to Louisa.

"In all the troubles of my life I never had one so hard to bear," Louisa wrote an aunt. She tried to continue working on her new book, *Jack and Jill*, to distract herself. But she was too overwhelmed with sorrow. There was only one bright spot: Before she died, May had made her sister-in-law promise to take the baby, nicknamed Lulu, to America.

She was to be raised by her Aunt Louisa.

In September 1880, ten-month-old Lulu arrived in Boston. Louisa was immediately enchanted by this yellow-haired, blue-eyed baby. She took her to Pinckney Street, on Beacon Hill in Boston, and set up a home with her. There they celebrated Lulu's first birthday, in November, in fine Alcott style. Crowned with greens, the baby was taken to the parlor and shown her tiny cake with one candle and a table full of gifts. Lulu's favorite present, as an artist's daughter and an author's niece, was a picture book.

Through Lulu, Louisa felt comforted for the loss of her sister. The blond, blue-eyed, fair-skinned child would often look at her exactly as May used to look. And Lulu was delightful in herself, healthy and spirited. Louisa couldn't take care of Lulu full time, because of her bad health, but fortunately she had the money to hire nurses and governesses.

Every summer Louisa took her niece to the seashore, at Nonquit on Buzzard's Bay. Louisa was delighted at the way Lulu strode into the water, as if she were going to wade all the way back to Europe. And the sight of Lulu trying to catch crabs made her laugh out loud. Although Louisa sometimes got weary of writing for the magazines, it was always a pleasure to make up stories to tell Lulu. Later, these tales were collected and published as *Lulu's Library*.

In April 1882, Ralph Emerson died. Many people mourned the Concord philosopher, but for the Alcotts it was a personal loss. "Our best and greatest American gone," wrote Louisa. "The nearest and dearest friend Father has ever had, and the man who has helped me most by his life, his books, his society."

That fall Bronson Alcott, who had always been in excellent health, suffered a stroke. Louisa spent more time in Concord, although she couldn't nurse him herself. This frustrated her badly, but she was almost fifty and not well.

Off and on, Louisa tried to work on *Jo's Boys*, a sequel to *Little Men*. It was hard going, partly because she couldn't bear to write about "Mrs. March" or "Amy," now that her mother and youngest sister were both gone. She explained this in the preface, when *Jo's Boys* was finally published in 1886.

Bronson Alcott got better, but he never fully recovered from his stroke. In the fall of 1885, Louisa finally decided to move the whole family—Bronson, Lulu, and Anna and her boys—from Concord into Boston, to a house in Louisburg Square. "I shall miss my quiet, carefree life in Boston," she wrote regretfully, "but it is best for all."

Ideas for more stories kept coming to Louisa's mind, but it was harder and harder for her to write. She was plagued by aching joints, nervousness, indigestion, dizziness, sleeplessness. Much as she loved her family, she craved peace and quiet. In December 1886, she moved into Dunreath Place, Dr. Rhoda Lawrence's rest home in Roxbury, outside of Boston.

In the quiet of Dunreath Place, under Dr. Lawrence's constant care, Louisa found some relief. But she often felt like "a sick oyster at low tide," as she put it. At fifty-five, Louisa looked seventy—gray-haired, wrinkled, bent over, and lame. She was bone weary, but she couldn't rest. She compromised by writing very slowly, only an hour or two a day.

These days, Louisa got so much mail that she couldn't answer all of it. But one letter she couldn't resist. It was from a boy who wanted to buy all of her books—and enclosed a quarter. Louisa wrote back, returning the boy's quarter and explaining that books cost much more than that. But she also sent him a copy of *Little Men*.

Louisa kept hoping that her health would

improve, if only she had the right treatment or enough rest. But she also worried about what would happen to her family if she did not recover. In the summer of 1887, she formally adopted her nephew John, now twenty-two, changing his last name to Alcott. If she died, John, her legal heir, would have the right to renew the copyright on her books and keep the income for the family.

Miss Alcott's readers were more eager than ever for more stories, more books. Louisa had ideas for a long book, but her doctor ordered her not to work on anything strenuous. However, she was still able to write an occasional story for *St. Nicholas* magazine. She sent her publisher a collection of stories for girls, and they were published as *A Garland for Girls* in November 1887.

Although her family was now financially secure, Louisa didn't feel that she could stop working. She worried about all the other needy people and good causes. When she

214

was too sick to write, she would sew—often clothes for orphans.

The day before Louisa's birthday that year, Anna brought Lulu to the rest home in Roxbury to deliver presents. "I heard Lulu rush up," Louisa wrote her sister afterward, "then, in the bed room she stopped & came in so quietly, looking so pale & excited I hardly knew her for my tornado. She fell upon me and we had our kisses first." Then two loads of birthday presents were brought in.

By February 1888, Louisa felt somewhat better, although not well enough to attend her nephew Frederick's wedding. But Anna told her all the details. Louisa could imagine her sister, mother of the groom, in her black lace over silk, and Lulu in pink silk, white lace, and rosebuds.

These days, Louisa felt hopeful of recovery. She was getting together stories for a third volume of *Lulu's Library*, and she wrote "Recollections of My Childhood" for the magazine *Youth's Companion*. For her young readers, and perhaps also herself, she remembered how Louy had tumbled into the Frog Pond on the Boston Common and been pulled out by a black boy. She became again, in her memory, the "wild" little girl who had run off for a day of fun and been discovered by the night watchman on a doorstep, asleep with a dog.

For Bronson Alcott, there was no doubt that the end was near. One springlike day early in March, Louisa took a carriage from Roxbury to Louisburg Square to see her father. She was sure this would be the last visit, although Bronson's smile was as serene as ever. Louisa knelt by his bed and said, "Father, here is your Louy. What are you thinking of as you lie here so happily?"

"I am going up," said her father, pointing upward. "Come with me."

"Oh, I wish I could," Louisa answered. She must have been thinking of all the dear people

Bronson expected to meet in the next life. Louisa also longed to see these people: Abby Alcott, Lizzie, and May; Ralph Emerson and Henry Thoreau.

The next morning, Louisa was overcome by violent pains in her head. She sank quickly into unconsciousness. When her father died on March 4, she could not be told.

On the afternoon of March 6, 1888, Louisa May Alcott died at the age of fifty-five. Thousands of people, across the United States and around the world, mourned the beloved author's death. But only a few of Louisa's family and close friends attended her funeral in Boston, according to her wishes. She was buried in the Sleepy Hollow Cemetery in Concord, next to her father, her mother, and her sister Lizzie.

Today, well over a century later, most of Louisa May Alcott's books are still in print. *Little Women*, especially, lives on not only as a book but on film. In the most recent movie version, Winona Ryder played Jo, Clare Danes was Beth, and Susan Sarandon, Mrs. March.

Young readers continue to open *Little Women* for the first time and meet the girls—Meg, Jo, Beth, and Amy—so much like the Alcott sisters. "We really lived it," remarked Louisa after writing the first volume of *Little Women*, "and if it succeeds that will be the reason of it." That was *half* the reason. The other half was that Louisa May Alcott, a writer of great power, made the girls live again in her stories.

Published works of Louisa May Alcott:

Flower Fables (1855)
Hospital Sketches (1863)
Moods (1864)
Little Women, Part I (1868)*
Little Women, Part II (1869)*
Old Fashioned Girl (1870)
Little Men (1871)
Work (1873)
Eight Cousins (1875)
Rose in Bloom (1876)
Under the Lilacs (1878)
Jack & Jill (1880)
Jo's Boys (1886)
Lulu's Library, Part I (1886)
A Garland for Girls (1887)
Lulu's Library, Part II (1887)
Lulu's Library, Part III (1889)

* both volumes now published as one